Nic was tense as he stood in the open-air courtyard in the middle of his *hacienda*-style home. His focus was on the imposing entrance doorway, which was still admitting a long line of glittering guests who had travelled from all over the world for this wine-tasting.

Hundreds of candles flickered in huge lanterns, waiters dressed immaculately in black and white moved among the guests offering wine and canapés. But all Nic could think was…would Maddie come? And why had he asked her, really?

Nic told himself it was because he wanted her gone. His belly clenched in rejection of that—it went much deeper. And he knew it. Really what he'd wanted since eight years ago, since he'd had that electric glimpse of her in a club in London, was to see her broken and contrite. To see that pale perfection undone.

Abby Green got hooked on Mills & Boon® romances while still in her teens, when she stumbled across one belonging to her grandmother in the west of Ireland. After many years of reading them voraciously, she sat down one day and gave it a go herself. Happily, after a few failed attempts, Mills & Boon bought her first manuscript.

Abby works freelance in the film and TV industry, but thankfully the four a.m. starts and the stresses of dealing with recalcitrant actors are becoming more and more infrequent, leaving her more time to write!

She loves to hear from readers, and you can contact her through her website at www.abby-green.com. She lives and works in Dublin.

Recent titles by the same author:

THE LEGEND OF DE MARCO
THE CALL OF THE DESERT
THE SULTAN'S CHOICE
SECRETS OF THE OASIS

**Did you know these are also available as eBooks?
Visit www.millsandboon.co.uk**

ONE NIGHT WITH THE ENEMY

BY
ABBY GREEN

First published in Great Britain 2012
by Mills & Boon, an imprint of Harlequin (UK) Limited.
Harlequin (UK) Limited, Eton House, 18-24 Paradise Road,
Richmond, Surrey TW9 1SR

ISBN: 978 0 263 22770 3

Harlequin (UK) policy is to use papers that are natural, renewable and recyclable products and made from wood grown in sustainable forests. The logging and manufacturing process conform to the legal environmental regulations of the country of origin.

Printed and bound in Great Britain
by CPI Antony Rowe, Chippenham, Wiltshire

ONE NIGHT
WITH THE ENEMY

This is for Michelle Lawlor, wine buff extraordinaire, with heartfelt thanks. Any errors are entirely my own!

I'd also like to dedicate this book to the memory of Penny Jordan. I am one of her many legions of fans who give thanks for her wonderful legacy.

CHAPTER ONE

MADDIE Vasquez stood in the shadows like a fugitive. Just yards away the plushest hotel in Mendoza rose in all its majestic colonial glory to face the imposing Plaza Indepencia. She reassured herself that she wasn't actually a fugitive. She was just collecting herself... She could see the calibre of the crowd going into the foyer: monied and exclusive. The elite of Mendoza society.

The evening was melting into night and lights twinkled in bushes and trees nearby, lending the scene a fairy-tale air. Maddie's soft mouth firmed and she tried to quell her staccato heartbeat. It had been a long time since she'd believed in fairy tales—if ever. She'd never harboured illusions about the dreamier side of life. A mother who saw you only as an accessory to be dressed up and paraded like a doll and a father who resented you for not being the son he'd lost would do that to a child.

Maddie shook her head, as if that could shake free the sudden melancholy assailing her, and at the same time her eye was caught by the almost silent arrival of a low-slung silver vehicle at the bottom of the main steps leading up to the hotel. Instinctively she drew back more. The car was clearly vintage and astronomically expensive. Her mouth dried and her palms grew sweaty—would it be...?

The door was opened by a uniformed hotel doorman and a tall shape uncurled from the driving seat.

It was him.

Her heart stopped beating for a long moment.

Nicolás Cristobal de Rojas. The most successful vintner in Mendoza—and probably all of Argentina by now. Not to mention his expansion into French Bordeaux country, which ensured he had two vintages a year. In the notoriously fickle world of winemaking the de Rojas estate profits had tripled and quadrupled in recent years, and success oozed from every inch of his six-foot-four, broad-shouldered frame.

He was dressed in a black tuxedo, and Maddie could see his gorgeous yet stern and arrogant features as he cast a bored-looking glance around him. It skipped over where she was hiding like a thief, and when he looked away her heart stuttered back to life.

She dragged in a breath. She'd forgotten how startling his blue eyes were. He looked leaner. Darker. Sexier. His distinctive dark blond hair had always made it easy to mark him out from the crowd—not that his sheer charisma and good looks wouldn't have marked him out anyway. He'd always been more than his looks…he'd always carried a tangible aura of power and sexual energy.

Another flash of movement made her drag her eyes away, and she saw a tall blonde beauty emerging from the other side of the car, helped by the conscientious doorman. As Maddie watched, the woman walked around to his side, her long fall of blonde hair shining almost as much as the floor-length silver lamé dress which outlined every slim curve of her body with a loving touch.

The woman linked her arm through his. Maddie couldn't see the look they shared, but from the smile on the woman's face she didn't doubt it was *hot.* A sudden shaft of physical pain lanced her and Maddie put a hand to her belly in reaction. *No,* she begged mentally. She didn't want him to affect her like this. She didn't want him to affect her at all.

She'd wasted long teenage years dreaming about him, lusting after him, building daydreams around him. And that foolish dreaming had culminated in catastrophe and a fresh deepening of the generations-old hostility between their families. It had caused the rift to end all rifts. It had broken her own family apart. She'd realised all of her most fervent fantasies—but had also been thrown into a nightmare of horrific revelations.

The last time she'd seen Nicolás Cristobal de Rojas had been a few years ago, in a club in London. Their eyes had clashed across the thronged room, and she'd never forget the look of pure loathing on his face before he'd turned away and disappeared.

Sucking in deep breaths and praying for control, Maddie squared her shoulders. She couldn't lurk in the shadows all night. She'd come to tell Nicolás Cristobal de Rojas that she was home and had no intention of selling out to him. Not now or ever. She held the long legacy of her family in her hands and it would not die with her. He had to know that—or he might put the same pressure on her as he'd done to her father, taking advantage of his physical and emotional weakness to encourage him to sell to his vastly more successful neighbour.

As much as she'd have loved to hide behind solicitors' letters, she couldn't afford to pay the legal fees. And she didn't want de Rojas to think she was too scared to confront him herself. She tried to block out the last cataclysmic meeting they'd had—if she went down that road now she'd turn around for sure. She had to focus on the present. And the future.

She knew better than anyone just how ruthless the de Rojas family could be, but even she had blanched at the pressure Nicolás de Rojas had put on an ailing man. It was the kind of thing she'd have expected of his father, but somehow, despite everything, not of Nicolás...*more fool her.* She of all people should have known what to expect.

With a shaking hand she smoothed down the glittery black dress she wore. Maddie's meagre budget since she'd left Argentina hadn't run to buying party dresses. Tonight was the prestigious annual Mendoza Vintners' Dinner, and she wouldn't have been able to get close to the place if she didn't look the part. Luckily she'd found some of her mother's dresses that her father hadn't destroyed in his rage eight years before...

At first it had looked modest enough—high-necked at the front. It was only when she'd had it on, aware that if she didn't leave soon she'd miss her window of opportunity, that she'd realised it was backless—to just above her buttocks. All her mother's other dresses needed serious dry-cleaning. This one had somehow miraculously been protected in a plastic covering. So it was this dress or nothing.

Maddie just wished that her mother had been less flamboyant—and taller. Maddie was five foot nine and the dress ended around her mid-thigh, showing lots of pale leg. Her unusual colouring of black hair, green eyes and pale skin was courtesy of a great-great-grandmother who had come to Argentina with a wave of Irish immigrants and subsequently married into the Vasquez family.

So now, as she finally stepped from the shadows outside the hotel and the gentle breeze whistled over her bare flesh, she felt ridiculously exposed. Mustering all the courage she would need for this encounter, she valiantly ignored the double-take glances of recognition she drew, and strode into the luxurious marbled lobby.

Nicolás Cristobal de Rojas stifled a yawn. He'd been working around the clock to ensure this year's grapes would be ready to pick soon. After a mercurial summer, they would either have one of the best vintages on their hands or the worst. He grimaced slightly. He knew bringing in his vintage wasn't the only excuse for driving himself like a demon. That work ethic was buried deep in his fraught childhood.

'Really, darling,' came a dry voice to his right, 'am I that boring?'

Nic forced his attention back into the room and looked down at his date. He quirked a mocking smile. 'Never.'

His blonde companion squeezed his arm playfully, 'I think the ennui is getting to you, Nic. You need to go to Buenos Aires and have some fun—I don't know how you stand it in this backwater.' She shuddered theatrically, then said something about going to the powder room and disappeared with a sexy sway to her walk.

Nic was relieved to be immune to this very feminine display, and watched as male heads swivelled to watch her progress. He shook his head ruefully and thanked his lucky stars that Estella's presence tonight might at least temporarily stave off the more determined of the Mendoza man-eaters. He was in no mood to humour the mercenary women he attracted in droves. His last lover had screamed hysterically at him for an hour and accused him of having no heart or soul. He had no desire to head down *that* path again any time soon.

He could do without sex if that was going to be the outcome. If truth be told, his last sexual encounters had all felt curiously…empty. Satisfying on one level only. And as for a more long-term relationship? He certainly had no intention of even thinking about that. The toxic relationship of his parents had cautioned him from an early age. He was going to choose a long-term partner with extreme care and diligence. Naturally there *would* be a long-term partner at some point in the future; he had a valuable legacy to pass on to the next generation, and he had no intention of breaking the precious cycle of inheritance.

Just then he saw a figure appear in the doorway to the ballroom. Inexplicably his skin tightened over his bones and the back of his neck prickled—the same way it had just now outside the hotel, when he'd felt as if he was being watched.

He couldn't make out the woman's features. He could only make out long, long shapely pale legs and a glittering short black dress which outlined a slender figure. But something about her was instantly *familiar.* In his gut. Midnight-black wavy hair was swept over one shoulder—and then he saw her head turn. Even from where he stood he could see a stillness enter her frame, and then she started to walk...directly towards him.

Ridiculously Nic felt the need to turn and leave. But he stood his ground. As she came closer and closer, weaving through the crowd, suspicion grew and formed in his head. *It couldn't be,* he told himself. *It's been years...she was in London.*

He was barely aware of the hushed murmurs surrounding him, growing louder as the woman finally came to a stop just a few feet away. Recognition and incredulity warred in his head. Along with the realisation that she was *stunning.* She had always been beautiful—slightly ethereal—but she'd matured into a true beauty since he'd seen her last. She was statuesque and slender and curvaceous all at once. An intoxicating package.

Nic hadn't even realised that he'd given her such a thorough examination until his eyes met hers and he saw the pink flush in her pale cheeks. It had a direct effect on his body, causing a hot throb of desire in his groin.

The ennui he'd just been teased about was long gone. Too many emotions and sensations were starting to fizz in his gut—the dominant ones being acrid betrayal and humiliation. *Still*, after all these years. He retreated behind a cold wall of anger. Anything to douse this very unwelcome stabbing of desire. His eyes narrowed and clashed with eyes so green they looked like jewels. He had to exert every ounce of his iron control not to be flung back into time and remember what it had felt like almost to drown in those eyes. The problem was he *had* drowned.

'Madalena Vasquez,' he drawled, not a hint of his loss of composure in his voice, 'what the hell are *you* doing here?'

Maddie winced inwardly and fought to retain her composure. She could remember a time when he'd called her Maddie. The walk from the door to here had felt as if it had taken years, not seconds, and hadn't been helped by the fact that her mother's shoes were a size too big. She was aware of the hush surrounding them, and the whispers—none of which she could imagine were complimentary after the very public way her father had thrown her and her mother out eight years before.

Nicolás de Rojas's mouth became a flat parody of a smile. 'Please accept my condolences on the death of your father.'

Fire flashed up Maddie's spine. 'Let's not pretend you care one iota,' she hissed, mindful of the eavesdroppers. Nicolás de Rojas didn't seem to be fazed by their audience at all, but the grief and futile anger she felt over her father's death nearly choked her.

The man in front of her folded his arms across his formidable chest, making him look even more intimidating. Maddie's skin itched uncomfortably where the dress revealed her back. Her hands were clenched to fists at her sides.

He shrugged negligently. 'No, I can't say I did care. But I can be polite at least.'

Maddie flushed at that. She'd seen in the papers that his father had died some years before. They were both products of generations who would have merrily danced on each other's graves, yet it wasn't in her to glory in someone's death—even an enemy's.

Awkwardly but sincerely, she said now, 'I'm sorry about your father too.'

He arched a brow and his face tightened. 'Are you going to extend that to my mother? She killed herself when she found out your mother and my father had had an affair for years…after your father told her.'

Maddie blanched to hear that Nicolás was aware of the affair. She saw in that instant how much anger his apparent civility was masking as his eyes flashed dangerously and white lines of tension bracketed his sensual mouth.

Her brain felt fuzzy. She shook her head. She'd had no idea her father had told his mother about the affair, or that she had taken her own life. 'I didn't know any of this…'

He dismissed her words with a slashing hand. 'You wouldn't, would you? You were so quick to leave and spend your family fortune running around Europe with your wastrel of a mother.'

Maddie felt sick. This was so much worse than she'd feared. She'd somehow naively imagined that she would say her few words to Nicolás de Rojas, he would respond with something at least civil, and that would be it. But the ancient feud between their families was alive and well and crackling between them—along with something else Maddie didn't want to acknowledge.

Suddenly Nicolás de Rojas cast a quick glance around them and emitted a guttural curse. He took Maddie's arm in one big hand. She was being summarily dragged to the other side of the room before she knew what was happening. He whirled her around to face him again in a quiet corner. This time all civility was stripped away, and his face was lean and stark with displeasure and anger.

Maddie yanked herself free and rubbed her tingling arm, determined not to let him see how shaken she was. 'How dare you treat me like some recalcitrant child!'

'I've asked you once already—what are you doing here, Vasquez? You're not welcome.'

Maddie felt anger surge up at his sheer arrogance and remembered why she was there and what was at stake: her entire livelihood. She stepped forward, dropping her hand. 'For your information I am just as welcome here as you, and I've come to tell you that my father didn't give in to your pressure to sell and neither will I.'

Nicolás de Rojas sneered. 'The only thing you own now is a piece of useless land full of gnarly vines. It's an eyesore. Your estate hasn't produced any wine of note for years.'

Maddie disguised the pain of knowing that her father had let it all go so spectacularly and spat back. 'You and your father systematically pushed and squeezed him out of the market until he couldn't possibly compete any more.'

His jaw clenched at that, and he bit out savagely, 'It's nothing more than was done to us time and time again. I'd love to tell you we spent all our time concocting ways to sabotage your business, but the Vasquez wines stopped selling because they were inferior—pure and simple. You did it to yourselves with no help from us.'

His words hit home with a dismaying ring of truth and Maddie took a hasty step back at his ferocity. She saw his eyes flash indignantly. Her reaction had more to do with his proximity and its effect on her body, and more disturbingly on her memories, than with his anger. She couldn't halt a vivid flashback to when she'd pressed herself so close against him she could feel every taut sinew and muscle. And the evidence of his arousal for her. It had been intoxicating, thrilling. She'd wanted him so badly she'd been begging him to—

'Here you are!'

Nic growled at the woman who had just appeared by their sides, 'Not now, Estella.'

Maddie sent up silent thanks for the interruption and cast a quick glance to see the gorgeous blonde who had been with Nicolás outside the hotel. She backed away but Nicolás grabbed her arm again.

'Estella, wait for me at the table,' he bit out.

The young woman looked from him to Maddie with wide eyes, and then whistled softly before walking away, shaking her head. Maddie dimly thought that she seemed very easy-going for a lover, but then Nicolás was clamping his hands on her arms. Angrily she pulled herself free again, feeling very raw after that too-vivid memory. She was vaguely aware of her dress slipping down over one shoulder as she pulled away, and saw Nicolás's eyes go there for a split second before something hot flashed in the blue depths.

Maddie spoke in a rush to stop herself responding to that look—which she *must* have imagined. This man felt nothing for her except hatred, pure and simple. 'I came to tell you that I'm back and I won't be selling the Vasquez estate. Even if I was do you really think I'd sell to a de Rojas after all we've been through? I'd burn it to the ground first. I intend to restore the Vasquez estate to its full glory.'

Nicolás stood tall, and then he barked out an incredulous laugh, head thrown back, revealing the strong column of his throat. When he looked down again Maddie felt a weakness invading her lower body—and a disturbing heat.

He shook his head. 'You must have done quite the number on your father before he died to get him to leave it to *you.* After you and your mother left and people heard of the affair, no one expected to see either of you back again. I think people would have expected him to leave it to a dog on the street rather than either one of you.'

Maddie's hands clenched. Pain bloomed inside her to think of that awful time and how angry her father had been—justifiably so. She gritted out, 'You have no idea what you're talking about.'

It was as if he didn't even hear her, though. He continued easily. 'It was common knowledge your father didn't have a *peso* to his name by the time he died. Is your mother's Swiss financier husband financing this whim?' His jaw tightened. 'Or perhaps you've bagged yourself a rich husband? Did you find one in London? You were frequenting the right clubs the last time I saw you.'

Maddie's insides burned with indignation. Her hands clenched even harder. 'No, my mother is *not* financing anything. And I don't have a rich husband, or boyfriend or lover. Not that it's any concern of yours.'

Mock shock and disbelief crossed Nicolás's face. 'You mean to tell me that the spoiled Vasquez princess thinks she can waltz back home and turn a bankrupt wine estate around with no help or expertise? Is this your new hobby because the Cannes yacht parties were becoming boring?'

Maddie felt the red tide of rage rise within her. He had no idea how badly she'd fought to prove herself to her fa-

ther—to prove that she could be as good as any man...
as good as her poor dead brother. She'd never have that
chance now, because he was dead too. And she would *not*
let the legacy she'd been bequeathed die with her. She had
to prove that she could do this. She would not let another
man stand in her way as her father had.

Passion resonated in her voice. 'That's exactly what I'm
saying, de Rojas. Stay out of my way and don't expect a
"For Sale" sign to go up—*ever.*'

Just as Maddie was backing away, wishing she wouldn't
have to present him with her naked back, he said chillingly,
'I'll give you two weeks until you run screaming out the
door. You have no idea what it takes to run a successful
wine business. You never worked a day in the vineyard
while you were growing up. It's been years since Vasquez
produced a wine worth mentioning, and your father got
carried away with his overpriced wines. You're in over
your head, Vasquez, and when you realise that it won't matter what price tag you put on that sign because I'll match
it. Purely because I would relish knowing that your family is gone from here for good.'

Maddie hid the dart of hurt; he knew that she'd never
worked a day in the vineyard because she'd told him once.
It had been intimate information which would now be
used against her.

He took a step closer and said chillingly, 'So you see,
eventually that estate will become part of the de Rojas
brand...and by denying it you're merely prolonging your
own misery. Just think—within a week you could be back
in London, sitting in the front row of a fashion show, with
enough money to keep you satisfied for a long time. I'll
personally see to it that you have no cause to return here
ever again.'

Maddie shook her head and tried to swallow the terrifying feeling of stepping off a ledge into the great un-known. She was hurt at the extent of this man's hostility. It hurt more than it should, and that scared her to death.

She couldn't help the emotional huskiness of her voice. 'This is my *home*—just as much as it's yours—and you will have to carry my dead body out before you get me to leave.'

Maddie was bitterly aware, despite her little assertion, that everything he said was right. Apart from his percep-tion of what her life was like. Of that he had no idea, and she wasn't about to enlighten him.

She backed away further and said, 'Don't come near my property, de Rojas…you or any of your people. You're not welcome.'

He smiled mockingly. 'I admire the act, Vasquez, and I look forward to seeing how long you can play the part.'

Maddie finally wrenched her gaze away from his and stalked off—but not before she almost stumbled in the too-big shoes. Gritting her teeth, she prayed silently all the way to the door that she would at least retain the dignity of not losing a shoe in front of the insufferably arrogant de Rojas and the gobsmacked crowd.

Maddie held her head high, and it was only when she finally reached her father's battered Jeep in the car park and locked herself inside that shock hit her and she shook uncontrollably for long minutes.

The awful reality was that he was right—she was on a hiding to nothing, trying to make their estate work again. But she'd be damned if she wasn't going to try. Her father had made long-overdue amends with Maddie, and even though it had come so late, Maddie had always clung to the hope that she would hear from her father. She would have returned here years ago if he'd welcomed her back.

For as long as she could remember she'd wanted nothing more than to work on the estate.

When she'd received the heartfelt letter from her ill father, with his outpouring of regret for his actions, Maddie hadn't been able to help but respond to his plea to come home to try to save their estate from oblivion.

Maddie's relationship with her father had never been close. He'd always made it clear he wanted sons, not a daughter, and had firmly believed that a woman's place was in the home and *not* in the business of winemaking. But he'd made up for a lifetime of dismissiveness while on his deathbed, when he'd realised he might lose everything.

Maddie had been hoping and praying she'd make it home in time to see him, but he'd passed away while she was in the air on her initial flight to Buenos Aires. His solicitor had met her with the news, and she'd gone straight from the airport in Mendoza to his private and lonely funeral in the small family graveyard in the grounds of their estate.

She hadn't even been able to get in touch with her mother, who was on a cruise somewhere with her fourth husband, who was some ten years her junior. She felt very alone now, when faced with the tangible animosity of Nicolás de Rojas and the seemingly insurmountable task of taking on the Vasquez estate.

Legend had it that Maddie's and Nicolás de Rojas's ancestors had been two Spanish friends, immigrants who'd made the long journey to Argentina to make new lives for themselves. They'd committed to setting up a vineyard together but something had happened—a woman had been involved: a love affair gone wrong and a bitter betrayal. As revenge Maddie's forefather had vowed to ruin the de Rojas name. So he'd founded Vasquez wines in direct competition and built it up right next door.

Vasquez wines had become ridiculously successful, decimating the de Rojas name, thus ensuring that the feud thrived and deepened as each generation fought for dominance and revenge. Violence between the families had been habitual, and once a member of the de Rojas family had even been murdered—although it had never been proved that the culprit had been a Vasquez.

Reversals in fortune had happened through the years, but by the time Maddie had been born the two estates had been almost neck and neck in terms of success. The generations-old dark cloud of hostility between the families seemed to have settled into an uneasy truce. In spite of the relative peace, though, Maddie had grown up knowing that she would be punished if she was caught even looking in the direction of the de Rojas vineyard.

Her cheeks stung with colour now when she recalled Nicolás's jeering *'princess'*. He'd only ever really seen her on the few social occasions when their families had been forced to mix, when hosts had nervously ensured that they didn't actually mingle.

Her mother had used those opportunities to parade Maddie in the latest fashions, forcing her naturally tomboyish and bookish daughter into the mould of the fashionable daughter she'd really wanted. Maddie's beautiful mother had wanted a confidante, not a child.

Maddie had been so mortified and uncomfortable in those situations that she'd done her best to fade into the background, while at the same time being aware of the very taboo fascination she felt for Nicolás Cristobal de Rojas, six years her senior, who even as a teenager had exuded unmistakable arrogance and virility. The tension and distance between their families had only made him more fascinating and alluring.

Then, as soon as she'd turned twelve, she'd been sent to

boarding school in England and had only returned home for the holidays. She'd lived for those few months, and had endured her mother's determination to parade her as if she was a doll just because it meant she could catch illicit glimpses of Nicolás de Rojas at the annual polo matches or the few social occasions their families shared. She'd look out of her bedroom window and sometimes would see him far in the distance on his horse as he inspected the neighbouring vineyard. To her, he'd looked like a golden-haired god. Strong and proud.

Whenever she'd seen him socially he'd always been surrounded by girls. Her mouth twisted when she thought of the beautiful blonde he'd so casually dismissed just now. Evidently nothing had changed there...

Eight years ago the uneasy truce between their families had exploded into bitterly fresh enmity and had shown Maddie the real depth of hatred between them. The fact that she'd actually challenged Nicolás's perception of her for a few days in time was something she had to forget. Because it had been undone as quickly as it had been done. What would someone like him be more likely to believe? A lifetime of propaganda and erroneous impressions? Or the briefest of moments fuelled by lust which had quickly been soured for ever?

Maddie shook her head and forced her trembling hand to start up the engine. She had just enough diesel to take her back to the small town of Villarosa, about thirty minutes outside Mendoza. No doubt someone of Nicolás's standing had a suite in the palatial hotel tonight, where he would be accompanied by his long-legged golden companion, but Maddie had nowhere to go except a crumbling homestead where the electricity had been cut off months ago and where she and a loyal skeleton staff depended on an ancient generator for power.

Maddie swung out of the hotel car park and reflected miserably that there must be plenty of de Rojas ancestors laughing down at her predicament right now.

CHAPTER TWO

Nic was stuck in a trance. All he could see in his mind's eye was the bared expanse of pale, slim back and the tumble of jet-black hair against her skin as Madalena Vasquez walked away. She'd stumbled slightly in her shoes, and it had made her look achingly vulnerable for a moment—before she'd recovered and swept out of the ballroom with all the hauteur of a queen. She'd had no right to look affronted at his taunting *'princess'*, for that was what she had always been.

When she'd been much younger she'd reminded him of a fragile porcelain doll, and he hated to admit it now but she'd always fascinated him with her unusually pale colouring and green eyes. There had been moments—the memory of which burned him now for his naivety—when he'd believed she'd been uncomfortable in their social milieu, when she'd looked almost sick as her mother pushed her to the fore. He'd sensed that beneath the delicate exterior lurked something much more solid.

Nic's mouth firmed. Well, he had first-hand experience of exactly how solid she was beneath that ethereal beauty. As if he needed to be reminded of the kind of person she was. Once she'd challenged his preconceptions of her, but it had all been an act.

She'd shared her mother's temptress nature—an earthy

sensuality that could ensnare the strongest of men. His heart thumped hard. It had ensnared his father before him, and then, a generation later, *him.* She'd only been seventeen. Humiliation burned Nic at recalling it, and he couldn't halt the flood of memories—not so soon after seeing her close up and in the flesh for the first time in years.

One evening he'd been inspecting the vines which were closest to the Vasquez estate; they always had to be ever vigilant in case of sabotage. That particular evening Nic had been weary and frustrated...weary of his mother's constant melancholy—never properly diagnosed as the depression it had been—and his father's caustic cruelty and habitual violence. At the dinner table his father had been drunkenly ranting about how the Vasquez run of success was threatening their sales. Nic had always firmly believed you made your own success, but, constrained by his authoritarian father, he hadn't been able to implement his own ideas.

Something had made Nic look up to the small hill which acted as a natural boundary between the two estates, and he'd seen a feminine figure with long black hair astride a huge stallion. *Madalena Vasquez.* Looking right at him.

His weariness had morphed instantly into burning irrational anger—at her for making him think about her, wonder about her, when she was forbidden. She also represented the dark and tangled feud which he had never really understood.

The supercilious image she presented on her horse had only galvanised him further and, giving in to an urge stronger than he'd been able to resist, Nic had spurred his horse to a canter and headed straight for her—only to see her whirl around and disappear.

He could still taste the urgency thrumming in his blood eight years later—to catch her and see her up close. Never once in their lives had they been allowed to speak to one another. Although he'd seen the way she would look at him from a distance and then glance away with artful shyness.

Finally he'd caught another glimpse of her, low down over her horse, hair streaming in the wind. She'd been cutting through the landscape like a bullet. With increasing urgency he'd thundered after her. It had been on the very edge of both their estates that he'd eventually seen her riderless horse, tied to a tree. She'd come to a remote part of their land where orchards had been planted. And then he'd seen her standing in a clearing of trees, as if she'd known he'd follow her.

More mesmerised by her flushed cheeks and that glossy fall of hair than he'd cared to admit, Nic had swung off his horse and come to stand in front of her. His anger had dissolved like snow on a hot stone. The very forbidden nature of what they were doing had infused the air around them.

'Why did you follow me?' she'd asked suddenly, her voice low and husky.

Nic had spoken on an unthinking reflex. 'Perhaps I just wanted to see the Vasquez princess up close.'

In that instant she went white as a ghost, her eyes like two huge wounded emeralds.

She backed away and Nic put out his hands, instantly contrite. 'Wait. Stop. I don't know why I said that... I'm sorry.' He took a breath. 'I followed you because I wanted to...and because I think you wanted me to.'

She'd flushed pink then, the colour rushing into her cheeks dramatically. Without even being aware of it Nic reached out a hand and touched her cheek, fascinated by the way her emotions showed so clearly, feeling its satiny texture beneath his callused palm. A shudder of pure longing went through him—so strong he nearly shook.

She stepped back, biting her lip, looking tortured. 'We shouldn't be here… If anyone sees us…'

Nic saw a tremor go through her slender frame, the way her young breasts pushed against the material of her shirt. Jodhpurs encased long, slim thighs.

He struggled with his control, waves of heat building inside him. She'd speared him with a defiant look then, which confirmed his suspicions that she wasn't as delicate as she had always appeared—as if her little gallop through the wilderness of their lands hadn't already told him that.

'I'm not a princess. I'm not like that. I hate being paraded in public like some kind of mannequin. It's my mother…she wishes I was more like her. They won't even let me go out riding unsupervised. I have to sneak out when they're busy…'

Nic saw her gaze fall to his mouth and her cheeks pinken again. Power and testosterone flooded his body, and he smiled wryly. 'I spend practically every waking hour on a horse…working in the vineyard.'

She looked back up at him, but not before torturing him with an innocently hungry look at his mouth.

'That's all I ever wanted. But when my brother died my father found me helping to pick the grapes one day and sent me inside. He told me that if he ever caught me in the vineyard again he'd take his belt to me.'

Nic winced and his stomach clenched. He knew only too well what the wrath of a father felt like. Gruffly he said, 'Your brother died a few years ago, didn't he?'

Madalena looked away, swallowing visibly before saying, 'He died in an accident when they were crushing the grapes. He was only thirteen.'

'I'm sorry.' And then he asked, a little wistfully, 'You were close?'

She looked back, her eyes suspiciously bright. 'I adored him. Our father was...*is*...prone to rages. One day I angered him, and he would have hit me but Alvaro stepped in and took it. My father wouldn't stop hitting him, enraged at being shown up by his own son. He was only eight at the time...'

Her eyes were swimming with tears. Nic had been the recipient of many a beating in his own time. Acting on an instinct too powerful to resist, he reached out and pulled her to him, enfolding her slim body in his, wrapping his arms around her. The need to comfort her was overwhelming, and completely alien for someone like him who generally held people at arm's length.

She was a complete stranger to him in so many ways, but in that moment he felt a deep kinship. After long moments she pulled back, and with the utmost reluctance Nic let her go.

She said shakily, 'I should go...they'll be looking for me...'

She turned and Nic reached out, gripping her arm with a desperate feeling in his belly. She looked back and he said, 'Wait...meet me here again tomorrow?'

The world seemed to stop turning for an infinitesimal moment, and Nic braced himself for a mocking laugh—some indication that he'd completely misread those few moments.

But Madalena's cheeks flushed red and she said huskily, 'I'd like that.'

They met every day for a week—stolen moments in that secret place where time seemed to be suspended in a bubble and where inhibitions fell away. Nic spoke to her of things he'd never told another soul as easily as if he hadn't experienced years of emotional isolation. Each day he became more and more consumed by Madalena

Vasquez. More and more entranced with her delicate beauty, which he'd discovered hid an earthy sensuality, driving him senseless with growing desire. Yet he managed not to touch her after that first day, when he'd pulled her into his arms to comfort her.

The depth of his need scared him, and the sensual and sexual tension building between them tipped over on that last day. When Nic arrived to find Maddie waiting, he didn't speak and nor did she. The air quivered and vibrated with awareness around them, and then she was in his arms before he'd stretched them out to pull her into them.

His mouth was on hers, and she was clutching him as if she were drowning. He sank a hand into her hair. It felt like liquid silk. He felt her legs shaking against his and slowly they lay down on the downy grass under the shade of the trees, oblivious to their idyllic surroundings. Heat consumed Nic so much that his hand trembled as he fumbled with the buttons on her blouse.

He was no callow, inexperienced youth, but he felt like one as she lay back and looked at him from under long, dark lashes, her cheeks stained red. When he'd opened her shirt and undid her bra to uncover pale breasts tipped with tight pink nipples, he nearly lost it completely.

He was drunk on her by then—drunk on the taste of those sweet breasts, and her soft mewling sounds of response and rolling hips—so he didn't hear anything until she tensed in his arms.

They both looked up at the same moment to see grim figures on horseback, staring down at them. It all became a blur as Nic scrambled to cover Maddie and she stood up behind him. Then they were both hauled unceremoniously out of the clearing by their respective estate employees and brought home...

'Hello? Earth to Nicolás?'

Nic flinched now, as if stung, and looked down to see Estella staring up at him.

She was holding two glasses of champagne. She handed one to him and said, 'Here. Looks like you could do with this.'

He was feeling incredibly raw and exposed, but he schooled his features and took the drink, restraining himself from downing it in one go.

'So, was that woman really one of the Vasquez family? I thought I might have to get a hose to cool things down between you.'

'She's the last Vasquez. She's come back to take over the family business,' Nic bit out tautly, wanting to rid himself of the potent images.

'That's interesting...' Estella mused in a far too innocent voice. 'You're the last in your line too...'

Nic glowered at Estella. 'The only thing interesting about it is that she'll be forced to sell that estate to me and we'll finally be rid of the Vasquez family for good.'

With tension radiating from his tall form he strode away from her and the speculative look on her face. The last thing Nic needed was someone analysing his encounter with Madalena Vasquez. And the last thing the de Rojas estate needed was for its name to be dragged back down into the mire of rumour and innuendo and a resumption of ancient hostilities. The sooner Madalena Vasquez realised the futility of her position and how unwelcome she was, the better for everyone.

'What the hell is he up to?' Maddie muttered to herself, and turned the silver embossed invitation over and back again, as if it might contain a booby trap.

The message was written on one side and simple.

You are cordially invited to a private tasting of this year's finest wines from the world-renowned de Rojas Estate.

Saturday, 7p.m., Casa de Rojas, Villarosa, Mendoza. Black Tie.

The invitation had arrived with that day's post, interrupting Maddie as she waded through her father's papers.

She heard a noise and looked up from where she was sitting at her father's study desk to see Hernan come in. He was their oldest and most loyal employee, her father's viticulturist, and his own father had been the viticulturist before him. He and his wife, Maria, who was the housekeeper, were both working for board alone, even though Maddie had told them she couldn't be sure when they might get paid again.

Her father's head winemaker had long since gone, and Maddie knew that she might have to take over that role until she could afford to hire someone new. Fresh from a degree in Oenology and Viticulture, she was lacking in practical experience but had a burning love for the industry and craved the opportunity. Even if it was a poisoned chalice.

She swallowed the emotion she felt at the evidence of Hernan's loyalty now and handed the card to him. He read it silently and handed it back with an inscrutable look on his face.

Maddie just arched a questioning brow.

After a long moment the old man said, 'You do know that if you accept the invitation you will be the first Vasquez to be invited onto de Rojas land since as far back as I can remember?'

Maddie nodded slowly. This was huge. And she had no

idea what he was playing at, but she had to admit she was intrigued to see the famed estate.

To her shock and surprise Hernan shrugged lightly. 'Perhaps you should go. Times have changed, and things can't go on as they always have. He's up to something. Of that I have no doubt. Nic de Rojas is infinitely more intelligent than his father, or even his father before him, so he is a dangerous enemy to have…but perhaps an enemy you know…?' He trailed off.

Maddie looked at the card thoughtfully. It had been two weeks exactly since her tumultuous meeting with Nicolás de Rojas, and she still felt shaky when she thought of it. Going through her father's papers since then had shown her the true ugly extent of how far Nicolás de Rojas was willing to go to to get his hands on their estate.

Her father had been bombarded with letter after letter advising him to sell up. Some had been cajoling, almost friendly in tone, and others had been downright threatening. They'd all been issued by the de Rojas solicitor but signed off with the arrogant Nicolás de Rojas scrawl. There'd even been a threatening letter dated the day her father had died.

As much as Maddie wanted to rip up the invitation and send it back in pieces to Nicolás, she knew she couldn't afford to isolate herself now. She needed to see what she was up against.

The party was the next evening.

She put the invitation in a drawer and stood up resolutely, clamping the gaucho hat she'd been wearing back on her head. 'I'll think about it. In the meantime we need to check the eastern vineyard again. It looks like our best prospect of a harvest this year.'

'You mean our *only* prospect,' Hernan said darkly as they walked out to the battered vineyard Jeep.

Maddie tried not to let the sensation of sheer panic overwhelm her. It was far too frequent for her liking, and not helped one bit by the realisation that the monumental task of harvesting their one chance of a wine that year was going to fall to her and Hernan and whatever friends and relations he could persuade to help with picking the grapes.

Her father had been a staunch old-school-style wine-maker, eschewing wholesale modern methods. That was all very well when you were producing top-of-the-line expensive wines in tandem with more affordable table wines, but in later years her father had all but stopped producing for the more accessible market.

Their one tiny glimmer of hope was in the grapes which had somehow survived the neglect of her father to flourish and ripen on the eastern slopes of the vineyard. These were the Sauvignon grapes which made the distinctive white wine which had put the Vasquez name on the map—particularly because red wines were more common in Argentina.

If they could harvest them, and assure investors of the quality and quantity, then perhaps someone would give them the money they needed to get back on track—or at the very least to be able to pay the basic bills again.

Nic was tense as he stood in the open-air courtyard in the middle of his *hacienda.* His focus was on the imposing entrance doorway, which was still admitting a long line of glittering guests who had travelled from all over the world for this tasting. Hundreds of candles flickered in huge lanterns, and waiters dressed immaculately in black and white moved among the guests offering wine and canapés. But all Nic could think was…*would she come? And why had he asked her, really?*

Nic told himself it was because he wanted her *gone.* His belly clenched. It went much deeper than that, and he knew it. Really, what he'd wanted since eight years ago, and since he'd had that electric glimpse of her in that club in London, was to see her broken and contrite. To see that pale perfection undone. To see her as humiliated as he'd felt. To see her as exposed. She'd lured him to expose himself and he'd stupidly believed the act she'd put on.

Her words resounded in his head. *'I was bored. OK? I wanted to seduce you because you were forbidden to me. It was exciting...'*

A smug voice came from his left. 'It'll only be a matter of time now before you can buy out the Vasquez estate.'

Nic took his eye off the door for a moment and looked at his solicitor, who had been a good friend of his parents. His mother's friend more than his father's. He was a small, overweight man, with mean, calculating eyes. Nic had never especially liked him, but it had been easier to retain him than to let him go after his father's death. He made a mental note to instruct his assistant to seek out new legal represention. He'd do his duty and give Señor Fiero a generous retirement package.

A movement at the door caught the corner of Nic's eye, and he looked back to see Madalena Vasquez entering. The instantaneous effect was almost laughable. His whole body tautened, and an urgent need to see her up close again rushed through him, shocking him with its force. He'd never felt that for another woman. Not even a lover.

From here she looked even more stunning than she had two weeks ago. Her hair was up and she was wearing a long midnight-blue sheath. Strapless, it showed off the delicate lines of her collarbone and shoulders. The gently muscled strength of her arms. There was something slightly odd about the dress, though, that he couldn't put his finger on. Much like the dress she'd worn the other night in Mendoza, it was as if it didn't fit perfectly. As if it wasn't hers.

He was so used to seeing women immaculately turned out that he could spot the slight anomaly a mile away, and it didn't fit with what he would have expected of Madalena Vasquez.

'Who is that? She looks familiar.'

'That,' Nic said tightly, irrationally not liking the fact that his solicitor was looking at her too, 'is Madalena Vasquez. She's home and taking over the family estate.'

The solicitor laughed cruelly. 'That place is a mess. She'll be begging you to buy her out.'

Nic moved away from his solicitor and towards Madalena. He couldn't fathom the urge he felt to turn around and punch the older man. It was visceral and disturbing, and the remnants of it lingered as he drew closer and saw that wide green gaze settle on him. Pink flooded her cheeks and he could see the faintest bruised colour under her eyes—signs of fatigue. His chest constricted. Once he'd believed in that artifice, but it was a trick to incur sympathy learnt from her mother. To make a man believe that she was as innocent as she looked. When she was rotten to the core.

Nevertheless his rogue body could not be dictated to by his mind. Desire was hot and instantaneous.

He put a smooth smile on his face and tried to ignore the increasing heat in his body. 'Welcome to my home.'

Maddie tried not to let Nicolás de Rojas see how affected she was just by watching him walk towards her. She felt like snorting incredulously. *Home* was a woeful understatement for this seriously palatial house. Once, a long time ago, her home had been as grand, but now it was a crumbling shell.

She didn't trust his urbane charm for a second. His eyes were like shards of ice and she shivered imperceptibly. Forgetting her resolve to appear nothing but aloof, she blurted out, 'Why did you invite me here?'

Quick as a shot he answered, 'Why did you come?'

Maddie flushed, all of her reasons for coming feeling very flimsy and transparent now. She should have just sent the invitation back in tiny pieces as she'd intended. But she hadn't.

She squared her shoulders. 'I came because it's been two weeks and I want to let you know that I've still no intention of going anywhere.'

Nicolás tipped his head slightly. She barely saw him make the gesture, and then a man appeared at his side.

'Yes, sir?'

'Madalena Vasquez, I'd like to introduce you to my house manager, Geraldo. He will show you around and see that you have everything you need. If you wouldn't mind excusing me? I have some new guests to attend to.'

And just like that he had turned and was walking away. Maddie felt inexplicably bereft, dropped...

The intensity of emotion he aroused so effortlessly was still high. Maddie cursed herself for allowing any hint of vulnerability through. She had to be strong enough to withstand Nicolás de Rojas and his brand of arrogance or she'd never survive.

She turned to the man waiting by her side with a big forced smile. 'Thank you.'

Maddie's head was spinning by the time Geraldo, who had proved to be a charming host, showed her back into the main courtyard, which was now thronged with people. Men were in tuxedos and women glittered in long dresses and jewels.

The reality of the sheer opulence she'd just seen was

a little hard to take in. The home itself—the few main rooms she'd been shown—was exquisitely furnished but also comfortable. Accessible. It was a *home.* And that had affected her deeply. Her own home had always been more like a cold and austere show house, full of dusty antiques. Unfortunately all of them had long since been sold to fund her father's downward spiral.

'I'll leave you here now...if that's okay?'

Maddie swung her gaze back to the pleasant house manager and realised he was waiting for her answer. 'Of course. You must be busy. I'm sorry to have taken you away from your duties.'

He said urbanely, 'It was a pleasure, Señorita Vasquez. Eduardo, who is our head winemaker, will see to it that you taste from the best of our selection of wines tonight.'

Another equally pleasant man was waiting to escort Maddie over to where the wine-tasting tables had been set up. It was only when she looked up and caught the coolly sardonic expression on Nicolás's face, where he stood head and shoulders above the crowd across the room, that she understood she was being effectively herded in exactly the direction he wanted her to go. And being shown exactly what he wanted her to see.

The transparency of his actions and the way she'd almost forgotten what was happening here galled her. So she merely skated her own gaze past his and made Eduardo the focus of her attention as he explained the various wines to her.

After a few minutes Maddie managed to take advantage of someone coming up to ask Eduardo a question and escape, turning instinctively away from the direction where Nicolás de Rojas was holding court with a rapt crowd. She hated being so aware of where he was at any moment, as if some kind of invisible cord linked her to him. And yet, a small snide voice reminded her, as soon as puberty had hit she'd had that awareness of him as a man.

She walked through a silent, dimly lit room full of luxuriously stuffed couches and rosewood furniture and out onto a blissfully quiet decked area which hugged the outside of the house. Little pools of golden light spilled out onto the ground, and Maddie went and curled her hands over the wooden fence which acted as a perimeter.

The strains of a jazz band playing for the very select crowd wafted through on the breeze. She smiled cynically. Nicolás de Rojas could have stopped her at the front door and she would have already been in awe of his screaming success and wealth.

The wide gravelled drive, the rows upon rows of well-tended fertile vines and gleaming outbuildings had been enough of a display. That was what she wanted for her own estate—to see it flourishing as it had when she was a young girl, with rows of vines full of plump sun-ripened grapes…

She heard a noise and whirled around. Her heart thumped hard in her chest at the sight of Nicolás de Rojas in the doorway of the room behind her, shoulders blocking out the light, hands in pockets. He was so rakishly handsome that for a moment she forgot about everything and could only see him.

Maddie called up every shred of self-control and smiled. But it was brittle. Seeing Nicolás's house up close like this had affected her far more deeply than she liked to admit.

'Did you really think that showing off your success would make me scurry to the nearest airport with my tail between my legs?'

His jaw was gritted but he stepped out of the doorway, making Maddie's breath hitch in her throat when his scent reached out and wound around her. She couldn't back away. The wooden posts were already digging into her soft flesh.

'It must feel very dull here after the bright lights of London...not to mention the ski slopes of Gstaad. Aren't you missing the season?'

Maddie flushed deep red. She smiled even harder, hiding the hurt at that particular memory. 'I wouldn't have had you down as a *Celebrity Now!* reader, Mr de Rojas.'

Maddie had long since berated herself that she should have been suspicious when her flighty mother had expressed a desire to see her—even offering to fly her out to meet her in the wealthy ski resort for a holiday. This was the same mother who had refused to help Maddie out because she believed that she'd already sacrificed enough for her daughter.

As soon as she'd arrived at the ski resort it had become apparent that her mother needed her daughter to help foster an image of dutiful motherhood. She'd been intent on seducing her current husband, who was divorced, but a committed and devoted father. Maddie had been too disappointed and heartsore to fight with her mother, and had given in to a cloying magazine shoot in which for all the world they'd appeared the best of friends.

Nicolás answered easily, 'I happened to be on a plane on my way home from Europe. The air hostess handed me the wrong magazine, but when I saw who was gracing the cover I couldn't resist reading all about your *wonderful* relationship with your mother and how you've both moved on *so well* from the painful split with your father.'

Maddie felt sick. She'd read the article too, and couldn't believe she'd been so hungry for affection that she'd let her mother manipulate her so crassly. She pushed the painful reality of her mother's selfishness aside.

'This evening was a wasted exercise on your part, de

Rojas. You've merely made me even more determined to succeed.'

The fact that he thought he had her so neatly boxed up and judged made fresh anger surge up inside Maddie.

'I've just spent two weeks in a house with no electricity, and as you can see I'm not running screaming for the nearest luxury health spa. Now, if you don't mind, it's late and I've got to be up early in the morning.'

Maddie gathered up her dress to stalk off, but at that moment one of her oversized shoes came off and she stumbled. A strong hand closed around one bare arm to steady her and the sensation was electric.

Nicolás didn't let her go, though. She was whirled around to face him again, one shoe on, one shoe off.

He was frowning down at her. 'What do you mean no electricity?'

Maddie was used to being considered tall, but right now she felt positively petite. Bitterness laced her voice at being made to feel so vulnerable, when she had no doubt that was exactly what this man had intended all along. 'We've been using an ancient generator to get electricity in our house since they cut my father off months ago—when he stopped paying the bills.'

Nicolás shook his head. He looked shocked. 'I didn't know it was that bad.'

Maddie tried to pull her arm back but his grip was firm. Panic at her helpless physical reaction galvanised her to say, 'As if you care. You were too busy signing off on your solicitor's letters, doing your utmost to get a dying man to sell up. Do you know that he received the last letter the day he died?'

Now Nicolás looked confused. His hand tightened. 'What are you talking about? I never signed any letters. Any correspondence between my family and yours stopped when my father died. I was too busy rebuilding our own brand and renovating the estate and house.'

'You can spout all the lies you like, de Rojas. This evening was a mistake. I've let down every generation of my family and my father by coming here. It won't happen again.'

Nicolás's hand softened its grip on her arm and Maddie felt ridiculously disorientated, her anger dissipating like mist over a hill. His eyes were intense blue flames that communicated something base and carnal directly to her insides.

His voice was deep. 'But you did come here tonight, and there's something in the air...it brought us together before, and it's still there.'

Maddie felt the sense of disorientation increase. She finally yanked her arm free from his grip, but his words were hurtling her back in time to when he had stood in front of her and said, *'You're nothing but a tempting tease. I was curious to know what the Vasquez princess tasted like and now I know—poisonous.'*

The bitterness and anger of that exchange eight years ago was far too acute, eclipsing everything else. Maddie had not trusted herself with another man since then because of it. She'd held a part of herself private and aloof for fear of getting hurt again, or facing painful revelations. She had to push him back before he guessed how vulnerable she was.

She squared her shoulders and forced herself to look Nicolás dead in the eye. 'I seduced you once, de Rojas. Did you really think this evening would induce me to try and seduce you again? Eight years isn't enough time for you to get over your wounded ego?'

Nicolás stood tall, and she saw him pale beneath his tan. 'You little bitch.'

CHAPTER THREE

MADDIE didn't know where on earth she'd got the nerve to say those words when, if anything, they could be more legitimately levelled at her. She hadn't got over what had happened eight years ago—not by a long shot.

She heard a rushing in her ears, but she ignored it and tossed her head. 'Don't worry. You won't see me again. I think we can safely say this farce is over. I came tonight because I was curious to see what you were up to. You've seriously underestimated me.'

She was turning away again when she forgot that she still had one shoe off. She stumbled into thin air, and would have fallen if Nicolás hadn't caught her and hauled her back against him. One strong arm was wrapped around her ribcage, just under her breasts, and the other was across her shoulders. Adrenalin pumped through Maddie's veins. She immediately tried to remove his arms but they were like steel bands. And they were completely alone.

She had an urge to shout out, but a hand came over her mouth as if he'd read her mind. Panic gripped her— not at the threat of violence but at the threat of something much more potent. The evidence of Nicolás de Rojas's hardening body at her back was liquefying her insides. A silent scream sounded in Maddie's head: *No! Not this, please.* He would expose her vulnerability in seconds if he touched her.

She bit down on the fleshy part of his hand and heard him curse—but not before she'd tasted the salty tang of his skin. Her belly swooped and fire danced along her veins. He moved her effortlessly in his arms and now she was facing him, his arms manacling her to his body, her hands behind her back. She was completely powerless. And, to her absolute disgust, the predominant thing she was feeling was excitement.

'Let me *go.*'

He shook his head, eyes glittering down into hers. Maddie felt as if she'd completely lost her footing. Past and present, everything was mixing, and she felt seriously overwhelmed.

'I'm not finished with you, Maddie.'

Maddie's heart lurched painfully at hearing him use the diminutive of her name. She could remember with painful clarity telling him that she preferred Maddie to the more stuffy-sounding Madalena. He had touched her cheek and said, 'Maddie it is, then…'

He smiled, and it was the smile of a predator, forcing Maddie back to the present moment. 'One thing you should know is that if I've underestimated you, then you've *seriously* underestimated *me.* We have unfinished business—and ironically enough it's got nothing to do with business.'

Before Maddie had even properly taken in his words or read his intent he'd hauled her even closer. His head descended and his hard mouth pressed against hers. For a second Maddie had no reaction except numb shock. And then sensation exploded behind her eyes—hot and urgent.

Desperately she tried to cling onto reality and not let that hot urgency take over her need to stay immobile and

unresponsive. But she might as well have been hoping that
the sun wouldn't rise in the morning.

Being in this man's arms again was like seeing a bea-
con of light strobing across a choppy ocean and reacting
to it with an unthinking instinct to seek harbour. Maddie
felt the inexorable and overpowering urge to follow it,
even as everything rational was screaming at her to stop,
pull herself free, not to react. But a much bigger part of
her was aching all over with the effort it took not to react.

As if sensing her turmoil, Nic freed her hands and lifted
his own to her head, fingers caressing her skull, angling
her head so that he could better plunder her mouth. His
tongue flicked against the closed seam of her lips and at
that touch Maddie felt her resistance falling away. Her
free hands hovered for a long moment. She knew in some
dim place that she should use them to push him away, but
when she put them between their bodies and felt the taut
musculature of his torso underneath his thin shirt they
clung...didn't push.

He growled low in his throat at her capitulation and became bolder, his tongue prising open her soft lips to seek
the hot interior of her mouth. The devastation of that simple intimacy made Maddie sway against him. She could
feel her breasts crushed against the solid wall of his chest.

One of his hands was on her waist, digging into her
flesh, anchoring her solidly against him. She could feel the
bold thrust of his arousal against her belly, and between
her legs she felt hot and moist.

The world was turning into a hot furnace of sensation
and desperate wanting—and then suddenly a cool breeze
was waking Maddie as if from a drugged trance and she
was blinking up into Nic's impassive face. It looked as if
it was carved from stone. Maddie felt like jelly. Her mouth

was swollen, her heart beating like a piston. Her hair was tumbling down over sensitised skin.

'You...' She couldn't even formulate a word beyond that.

In a voice so cold it woke her up more effectively than anything else, Nic said, 'What do you want to say, Maddie? You want me to believe this act? That I've effectively rendered you speechless with passion?'

A look crossed his face that was so bitter it took Maddie aback. For a moment she was distracted from her growing humiliation.

'You forget that you already tried that once with me. I'm not stupid enough to fall for it again. You can't, however, deny that you want me. As much if not more than when you were hot and trembling in my arms eight years ago. I could have taken you that day and you would have been with me every step of the way. You might have seduced me out of boredom, but there was nothing bored about your response then—or just now. And you've never been able to handle that reality.'

The sheer arrogance of his tone and expression revived Maddie from the fugue she'd been in. She moved out of his embrace with a jerky movement and saw dark colour flash along his cheekbones.

'I am not interested in your hypotheses, or your take on the past. The past is in the past and that's where it'll stay. *This...*' she waved a hand to encompass what had just happened '...is nothing but evidence that physical chemistry can be dismayingly arbitrary. That's *all.*'

Nic smiled. 'If I hadn't stopped when I had I could be taking you right here, just feet away from one hundred guests, and I'd have had to put a hand over your mouth to stifle your screams of pleasure.'

The sheer carnality of his words made Maddie raise her hand—he'd pushed her too far.

Before it could connect to his smug face he'd caught it in a steel-fingered grip. Shock washed through Maddie in a wave. She'd never raised a hand to anyone in her life. The line of Nic's mouth was impossibly grim.

'I was merely proving that you're no more in control of your desire for me now than you were eight years ago, no matter how much you tried to convince me that you'd found what we had done so abhorrent it made you physically ill. You came here tonight to test me as much as I tested you. My bed is free at the moment...you're more than welcome to join me there and we can indulge this *arbitrary chemistry* until you've come to your senses and decided to sell the Vasquez estate to me.'

Maddie ripped her hand free of his grip and had to curb the urge to try and strike him again. His version of what had happened that cataclysmic afternoon was very different from hers. She knew she'd given him the impression that what they'd shared had disgusted her...and for a while she *had* found what they'd done abhorrent. But not for the reasons he obviously believed.

And she couldn't tell him. As much as she hated him right now, telling him the truth would only expose her even more. He would know that that week had meant everything to her, that she hadn't set out coldly to seduce him just for her amusement. There was no way she could disabuse him of that belief now. It was her only defence against him.

She stood very tall and said frostily, 'You seem to have forgotten that your bed was busy enough only two weeks ago. I think I'll pass, thanks.'

And then she turned and walked out.

To her intense relief he didn't stop her. It was only when she got outside to the main door that Maddie realised that she was barefoot. She certainly wasn't going to go back now for her shoes and risk seeing Nic again. She scrambled into the Jeep as soon as the valet brought it round, and as she saw the lights of the *hacienda* grow smaller in her rearview mirror she finally let out her breath.

She'd been a prize fool to think that Nic de Rojas wouldn't bring up what had happened in the past. He was a very virile and proud man. She knew she'd damaged his ego then...and she shuddered now when she recalled the bitter look she'd seen cross his face just a short while ago. She'd had no idea it would all feel so fresh and unresolved between them.

Even though the events of eight years before had sent out violent ripples, she would have imagined that the actual week which had led to those events had faded in his memory. That the intervening years and the countless affairs he seemed to have had with beautiful women would have made Maddie's innocent and gauche charms fade into insignificance...

The way he'd just kissed her, together with the memory of that week—those heady days when desire had tightened like a steel coil in her belly until she'd begged him to make love to her—made Maddie shake so much that she had to pull over on the hard shoulder or risk a crash. She put her head down on the steering wheel between her hands and tried to empty her mind, but it was impossible... the memories were too potent—especially after what had just happened.

She'd managed to evade her mother and father that day, and take a horse out riding on her own. She'd always instinctively hoped for a glimpse of Nic de Rojas on his own estate, and her heart had almost stopped when she'd seen him just metres away. The intensity on his face had scared her and she'd turned her horse to run, not even sure what she was running from. Perhaps it had been the delicious and illicit excitement thrumming through her blood.

She could remember looking back and seeing that he was following with that same intense expression—and her excitement had spiked to almost unbearable levels. Her whole body had gone on fire. The friction of the horse as it had surged powerfully between her legs had nearly made her cry out she was so oversensitised. By the time she'd reached the remote orchard which straddled both their estates her body had been as taut as a bowstring, humming for him.

That orchard was a favourite spot of hers. A secret place. And then he'd been there, swinging lithely off his horse, full of that taut energy. It had been overwhelming to see him up close at last—nothing could have prepared her for his sheer masculine perfection.

He'd touched her so gently. And they'd spoken. Really spoken. After years of feeling as if no one could possibly understand her Maddie had found a kinship with the most unlikely person: the son of her family's sworn enemies.

That first day when Maddie had tried to leave, her heart had felt heavier than a stone in her chest. Until Nic had asked to see her again the following day. And then the next and the next.

The week had taken on an unreal aspect...dreamy. Those illicit moments under the spreading branches of the orchard trees had become the only reality Maddie wanted. Nic had consumed her, filled her nights with vivid and carnal dreams. By the end of the week she'd been in such physical turmoil—craving him but scared of that craving—that she'd all but thrown herself at him.

He'd kissed her and touched her, and Maddie's face flamed even now to remember the wanton way she'd writhed beneath his hands, begging for more of something she could only guess at.

And then all hell had broken loose.

Huge looming figures on horseback had appeared and smashed apart the idyll. Evidently their regular absences had been noted by keen eyes. Nic had put Maddie behind him and she could remember doing up her shirt with numb hands, panic-stricken as she'd heard the shouts get louder. And then they'd both been hauled out of the trees and marched away. Maddie could remember looking back to see Nic being corralled onto his stallion, flinging his father's men off him, snarling at them.

She'd sobbed out loud when she'd seen one of the men land him a blow to stop him hitting out. But by then she'd been unceremoniously dumped onto her own horse and was being led away.

By the time she'd got home her mother had been waiting, white-faced and seethingly angry. She'd asked, 'Is it true? You were found with Nicolás de Rojas?'

For the first time in her life Maddie had felt the fire of rebellion stir within her, and she had lifted her chin and answered in a strong voice, 'Yes, it's true.'

She'd not been prepared when her mother slapped her so hard across the face that her teeth had rattled in her head. She'd felt blood on the inside of her mouth. In shock she'd lifted a hand to her cheek and stared in horror at this woman who, at the most, had only ever touched her in public, to give an impression of a closeness that didn't exist.

Then her mother had broken down into hysterical tears. Before Maddie had known it, with her face still stinging hotly, she'd been leading her mother into the drawing room and forcing her to take some brandy to calm her down.

Eventually her mother had looked at her and shuddered expressively. Completely bewildered, Maddie had said,

'Mother, is it really so bad that I was with Nicolás? We… like each other.'

That had set her mother off again, and when she'd finally calmed down once more she'd pulled Maddie down onto the couch beside her. 'You cannot see him again, Madalena. I forbid it. Think of what it would do to your father.'

That rebellion stirred in Maddie's breast again—she could no more deny that she wanted to see Nic again than deny her own name. She stood up, agitated. 'That's ridiculous. You can't stop me seeing him. We don't care about the stupid feud. It's gone on long enough.'

Her mother stood up too. 'Madalena, you will *not* disobey me in this.'

Her mother's constant use of her full name, *Madalena*, broke something apart inside Maddie. Years of frustration at having to tiptoe around her father's mercurial moods, brought on by his abject grief for his dead son and her mother's blatant self-interest, made Maddie explode. 'If I want to see Nic de Rojas again there is nothing you can do to stop me.'

An awful stillness came into the room, and Maddie watched as her mother seemed to wither in front of her.

The glass in her hand was shaking so much that Maddie reached out and took it from her, saying with exasperation, 'Mother, your dramatics won't work with me. They might work on Father, but—'

'I'll tell you why you can't see him again.'

Maddie stopped talking. Something about the low tone of her mother's voice had made a shiver go down her spine. 'What are you talking about?'

And then her mother spoke—and broke Maddie's world into tiny pieces for ever.

'Ever since I was a young girl, when our families used

to socialise in Mendoza, I was in love with Sebastian de Rojas...' Her mother's mouth twisted. 'I wasn't from here, so I knew only the vaguest details about the feud between this family and his own...'

Maddie tried to make sense of what her mother had said. 'You were in love with Nicolás's father? But what's that got to do with anything now?'

Maddie's mother sat down again heavily, wringing her hands in her lap. She avoided Maddie's eyes. 'The truth is, I wanted Sebastian to marry *me*. But I was too young, and his family forced him to marry his wife because she'd been picked by his parents... He married her, and they had their son, Nicolás, very quickly.' Maddie's mother's voice broke. 'I thought he was lost to me for ever...until I met your father.' She looked up at Maddie, her eyes anguished. 'Part of the reason I married him was so I could be closer to Sebastian. When he saw me again he couldn't resist taking me back into his bed. We met in hotels, whenever we could...' Her mouth took on a bitter aspect for a moment. 'I wasn't under any illusions. Sebastian got a thrill out of taking the wife of his enemy to bed, but he'd never have jeopardised his reputation by revealing it.'

Maddie was feeling increasingly distant from everything, as if her mother's voice was coming from far away.

'He went to Europe one winter, to see about extending the business, and when he came back I was pregnant with Alvaro—your brother. He cut off all contact, believing that I'd turned my back on him, choosing my marriage over him.'

Maddie's mother's eyes swam with tears—but Maddie couldn't drum up any sympathy. She felt sick at learning the lengths to which her mother had gone just to get her own way. She'd married a man she didn't love just to entice another married man away from his wife and son.

'I don't see what any of this has to do with me not seeing Nic de Rojas again.' Maddie turned to leave the room and heard her mother standing behind her.

'It has *everything* to do with why you can't see him again.'

With the utmost reluctance Maddie stopped and turned around.

Her mother swallowed visibly. 'I didn't stop seeing Sebastian completely. There were a couple of times when I…I managed to persaude him to meet me.' Her mother took in a deep shuddery breath. 'After one of those times I fell pregnant…with you.' Maddie's mother's cheeks flared a deep and ugly red. 'But in that time I'd also slept with your father. The fact is that I can't be sure that Sebastian de Rojas isn't your father.'

Maddie looked at her mother. The words had hit an invisible wall and fallen somewhere between them, where she couldn't take in their horrible meaning.

Her mother seemed to realise that, and said harshly, 'You can't see Nicolás de Rojas again because he could be your half-brother.'

The glass Maddie had taken out of her mother's hand dropped out of hers to the parquet floor, shattering to pieces. She didn't even notice. Numb shock was enveloping her.

The only thing that broke through the shock and horror of her mother's revelations was the inarticulate roar of rage that came from behind them. Maddie's father stood in the doorway, red-faced, apoplectic. His eyes were mad, and he said in a choked voice, 'I knew it. I always knew there was something between you. Was my son even *my* son, or was he also the son of that bastard?'

Maddie's memory after that was hazy. She remembered a lot of shouting and crying. And being dragged roughly up to her room by her father and shut inside. The following day, after a sleepless night, Maddie had snuck out of her first-floor window and gone to find a horse. She hadn't even cared about her father's wrath any more. She'd needed to get out.

To her horror, she'd found that she'd instinctively made for the orchard again. Too overcome with everything, she'd slithered off her horse before she'd spotted that she wasn't alone. Nic de Rojas had stepped out from the shadows of the trees, his face grim.

Her belly had clenched painfully with a mixture of dread and that awful, illicit excitement. Had she been hoping that he would be here, as he had been every other day, despite what had happened? But what had felt so pure and right the previous day now felt tainted and wrong.

'Why are you here?'

He smiled but it was tight. 'I wanted to know if you'd come back.'

Seeing him here like this—when she carried such awful knowledge—was too much. Choking on the words, she said, 'I came to be alone, actually. I didn't want to see you.'

His face tightened and Maddie spoke quickly to stop him saying anything, 'You should leave. *Now.*'

He came up to her, put his hands on her arms. 'I don't believe that you don't want to see me. Are you going to let them intimidate you?'

His touch was too much. Maddie wrenched herself free, hysteria clawing upwards. 'Get your hands off me. I can't bear it if you touch me.'

She'd whirled away from him, bile rising uncontrollably. She was sick all over the grass where they'd lain the day before. Trembling all over, and icy cold, she stood up again to see a white-faced Nic looking at her.

'Please…just go. I don't want to see you again.'

'You could have fooled me yesterday.'

Bile rose again, and Maddie swallowed it down, saying thickly, 'That was yesterday. This is today. And I don't want anything to do with you again.'

He wasn't moving, and Maddie was becoming desperate. She couldn't bear to look at Nic. Not when he aroused such feelings in her, and not when he could possibly be—

Her stomach cramped with horror and she blurted out the first thing she could think of. 'I was bored, okay? I was bored and I wanted to see if I could seduce you. You were forbidden. It was exciting. That's *all*...'

Maddie lifted her heavy head from the steering wheel of the Jeep. The bright lights of a passing car made her wince. Her head felt thick from the onslaught of memories. She cut them off. She didn't need to remember the next bit—the way Nic had become so cold and dismissive. The way he'd told her that she'd tasted like poison.

He'd come close and said, with chilling emphasis, 'I used to think the feud was irrelevant...well, it's just become relevant again.'

Maddie had just wanted him gone, and when he'd finally left she'd sat down and cried and cried until she'd fallen into an exhausted sleep.

When she'd returned to the house hours later she'd found her bags packed and her father waiting with her mother by the car. Without even a word of explanation he'd driven them silently to the airport and left them there. He'd just said, 'You are no longer my wife and daughter.'

Maddie and her mother had boarded a flight to Buenos Aires. When they'd reached her aunt's house in the suburbs she'd turned to her mother and said, 'I want to know for sure who my father is. I think I deserve that much at least.'

Her mother, tight-lipped, had finally agreed, but one of the conditions of getting the DNA sample from her soon-to-be ex-husband had meant that she'd had to sacrifice a generous divorce settlement—something she'd never forgiven Maddie for.

A month after they'd left Mendoza and her home Maddie had gone to a doctor's office in Buenos Aires with the DNA sample and submitted to the test. Two weeks after that she'd got the results and found out that she wasn't remotely related to Nicolás de Rojas, or his father. She was, without a shadow of a doubt, a Vasquez.

The knowledge was cold comfort when she knew that she would take her mother's sordid revelations to her grave, along with the even more painful revelation that Nic had felt nothing more than lust for her. She'd believed that he'd shared an intimate part of himself with her, but it had all been an act to lull her into a false sense of security. When she thought of how beautifully he'd manipulated her, so that she'd been aching for him after only a few days, she felt shamed.

Maddie eventually felt strong enough to start up the Jeep again and continue the journey home. She'd written to her father to tell him about the DNA result, but he still hadn't forgiven her for the sins of her mother...until he'd been on his deathbed. Maddie had to honour his wishes now and do everything in her power to forget about Nic de Rojas and get on with saving the Vasquez estate.

'You left these behind last night, Cinderella.'

Maddie's back tensed at the all-too-familiar deep and drawling voice. Her skin prickled all over. Slowly she looked up from where she'd been inspecting the vines to see a tall dark shape silhouetted against the sun, holding out a pair of shoes.

For a second Maddie blinked uncomprehendingly. She'd hardly slept a wink last night, as every time she'd closed her eyes lurid images and nightmares had beckoned. So perhaps now she was hallucinating from tiredness.

When the shoes and the shape didn't disappear, Maddie scowled and stood up. Reaching for the shoes, she said stiffly, 'You really didn't need to go to the trouble.'

She was feeling dusty in worn jeans, a plain T-shirt and an old pair of riding boots. Thankfully the gaucho hat she wore shielded her from the intense blue of Nic's eyes as well as from the sun. She could see very well from under the shaded brim that he too was dressed casually, in a dark polo shirt and faded jeans which clung to powerful thigh muscles.

'I'm intrigued to know why you're wearing shoes and dresses a size too large.'

Maddie flushed and glared up at him from under the hat, not wholly surprised that he would know her shoe size. Her breath was taken away by his dynamic magnetism and the sheer force of seeing him in the daylight. The blue of his eyes was stark against the olive tones of his skin.

Without even thinking Maddie muttered, 'They're my mother's.'

He arched a brow. 'Your luggage got lost?'

Maddie started to move away from the intensity of his presence and said caustically, 'Yes—all twenty-four of my personally monogrammed designer cases.'

It was only then that she realised what she was doing— and Maddie suddenly realised the magnitude of Nic de Rojas seeing the exent of their pathetic crop. She whirled around to face him again. 'How did you get in here? You need to get off this land immediately. It's private property.'

He made a tutting sound and folded his arms, drawing Maddie's eye effortlessly to his impressive muscles. She looked back up, angry with herself for being so weak.

'*So* rude! And when I went out of my way to show

you such hospitality last night… We're making history, Maddie. The first time anyone in our families has breached the divide.' Then his mouth flattened. 'Apart from your mother and my father's sordid affair, of course, and our own…*unsatisfactory* foray following in their footsteps.'

Maddie felt sick and avoided his eyes. 'That was a long time ago.' She lifted her chin, but something in Nic's face had hardened, and Maddie shivered slightly.

'You're quite the enigma, aren't you, Madalena Vasquez? Somehow I can't really see you as the studious type.'

Maddie went cold for a second, and then recalled her conversation with his head winemaker, Eduardo. Bitterly she remarked, 'You got your employees to report back on our conversations? Or did you bug them and listen in?'

Nic was even more incredulous. 'You're *really* claiming that you did a degree in Oenology and Vitculture in between your frantic socialising?'

Incensed, Maddie hit back, 'Your own hectic social life didn't seem to prevent *you* from becoming one of the youngest Masters of Wine in the world.'

His eyes flashed. 'Been keeping tabs on me, Maddie?'

Maddie flushed and looked down again, and then a deep inner pride made her look back up. She wouldn't let him cow her. She lifted her chin defiantly. 'It's true. I graduated last year with a first-class degree. You can check the University of Bordeaux's records if you don't believe me.'

'Who funded your studies, Maddie? A generous lover? Or perhaps you seduced your way to gaining a First?'

CHAPTER FOUR

MADDIE shook with impotent rage. 'That's right, Nic. I seduced my teachers and lecturers into giving me the degree.
I'm *that* good in bed, and they're *that* corrupt.'

Nic flushed. He'd never normally goad a woman like
this. But no other woman pushed his buttons like this one
did. The problem was that this knowledge was turning everything on its head. If she had indeed graduated with a
First from Bordeaux University, it was exploding most of
his firmly entrenched opinions of Maddie Vasquez.

Uncomfortable now, he asked, 'Is that where all your
money went?'

For a moment it looked as if she wouldn't answer, and
on some level Nic couldn't blame her. But then she did.
Her voice was stiff.

'I was working on a vineyard in Bordeaux, and the
owner there sponsored me through the course.'

She was avoiding his eye. Nic longed to tip her chin up
so he could see her eyes but he was afraid to touch her.
Afraid that after losing control as he had last night he'd
lose it again and have her on her back on the ground right
here under the vines.

She looked at him then, and her eyes were spitting green
sparks. 'And before you ask—no, I did not sleep with the
owner to get him to sponsor me. He runs a scholarship pro-

gram in tandem with the University of Bordeaux to educate his employees and I qualified for it. It's as simple as that.'

'Lucky you, indeed,' Nic drawled, but desire was an insistent beat inside him, distracting him from these revelations. Maddie's breasts pushed against the fabric of her T-shirt. He could see a sliver of pale skin at her waist, where her top had come untucked from her jeans. Her hair was in a long plait, with loose tendrils trailing over her shoulders and stuck to her hot cheeks. She was more beautiful than any woman he'd seen in a long time. If ever. Something inside his chest twisted painfully.

Last night when he'd held her against him he'd known a large part of giving in to his desire was to prove a point to himself. He'd needed to see her undone. And she had been—she'd been swaying like a drunk person after that kiss. It had taken all of his self-control to appear coherent when his own head had been scrambled to pieces and all he'd wanted was to tip her over his shoulder and carry her to his bedroom like some caveman.

And, while it had made a dark satisfaction go through him to know that she did desire him, it hadn't been half as satisfying as he'd expected. Because he wanted more. Much more. He wanted the ultimate fulfilment of knowing this woman intimately. He wanted to finish what had started that week eight years ago.

Why was he looking as her so assessingly? Maddie didn't like it at all—or the way he seemed perfectly comfortable in her territory.

She crossed her arms over her chest. 'I want you to leave—*now*. You're not welcome here.'

His eyes narrowed on her as if he'd just thought of something. His voice was grim. 'I want to see those letters. The ones you said were signed by me.'

Maddie hadn't expected that. She opened and closed her

mouth, and then realised that she had no reason to deny him this. And it would get him away from the vineyard. 'Fine,' she said stiffly. 'They're at the house.'

She turned and walked to the edge of the row of vines, very aware of Nic behind her. She could see Hernan in the distance, inspecting another row of vines. He made a face, but Maddie just sent him a signal that she was okay. She saw Nic's gleaming Jeep parked alongside her battered one. Naturally he opened the passenger door of his own Jeep, and after a brief internal struggle Maddie took off her hat and got in.

Nic sent an expressive glance to her Jeep and muttered, as he turned and drove away, 'That thing is a death trap.'

Maddie smiled sweetly at his profile. 'Of which you must thoroughly approve.'

He sent her a dark glance, his jaw clenched. 'I don't wish you *dead*, Maddie, just gone. There's a big difference.' He shifted gears expertly and then asked, 'So, how long were you in France?'

Maddie hesitated before answering, loath to reveal anything of her personal life. 'I went there when I was twenty-one, after spending a year in London.'

Nic's mouth tightened. 'That would have been when I saw you in that nightclub.'

Maddie almost flinched when she thought of the disgust on his face that night, as his scathing gaze had raked her up and down before he'd turned on his heel and walked out with a bevy of beauties in his wake. She longed to tell him that she'd only been there because she'd bumped into some old friends from her English school days and they'd insisted that she go with them to celebrate the birthday of a friend.

They'd even loaned her clothes—which was why she'd been wearing a silver lamé sheath which had not left much to the imagination. She had to concede now that she didn't seem to have much luck with clothes around Nic de Rojas.

All she said, though in a slightly defeated voice, was 'Yes.' And she looked out of the window, missing the quick speculative glance Nic sent her.

Nic studied her profile and had the strong suspicion that she was holding something back—but what? Evidently she'd partied hard for a year in London and then moved to France to work on a vineyard. Maybe her money had run out and she'd been forced to that decision? It didn't quite fit, but perhaps she'd decided the bigger prize would be to come home and take over the business.

And perhaps he had underestimated her ambition. He remembered how wistful she'd been when she'd told him that she'd always wanted to work in the vineyard. He'd dismissed it eight years ago as part of her act, but had to concede now that if she had indeed completed a degree in Oenology and Viticulture then she must be more dedicated than he'd given her credit for.

Certainly she was still here and not running for the hills, as she'd pointed out. And she'd been on hands and knees in the earth just now, unafraid to get dirty. He had to admit that he was shocked at the evidence of how rundown the Vasquez estate had become. He'd seen the faint purple bruises of fatigue under Maddie's eyes which her makeup had failed to hide completely last night. What he didn't like was the protective feeling that had struck him when he noticed them.

They were in front of the villa now. It was crumbling, but still held the faded grandeur of its heyday. The reversal of fortune between the two estates was stark now, but Nic ruthlessly pushed down that insidiously lingering protective feeling and got out. There was no sense of triumph at all, which surprised him slightly. He waited for Maddie to lead him into the house.

'Maria, would you mind bringing some coffee, please?'

Maddie sent up silent thanks that Maria was there to greet them. The older woman bustled off again, for all the world as if this were a usual occurrence and she still had her normal job as housekeeper and all that it entailed. It was important for Maddie not to let Nic see how bad things were. If she could maintain an impression of some kind of normality then he might not circle them like a vulture over a dead carcass. She'd given far too much away last night—in more ways than one.

Colour flared into her cheeks at the thought of that kiss, and Maddie showed Nic into the bright yet dusty study, hoping he wouldn't notice. She went straight to her father's ancient heavy oak desk, took out the letters and handed them to him silently, curious as to his reaction. Maria came back with the coffee and Maddie served. Nic had sat down, and was opening the letters and reading them.

Maddie sat down on the other side of the desk and only realised then how shaky her legs were. So far his face was impassive, but when he got to the last letter his nostrils flared and colour tinged his cheekbones. Maddie's stomach tensed. She could sense his anger already.

Finally he looked at her. 'That's not my signature.'

She frowned. 'It's your name on the bottom.'

'I know,' he said grimly. 'But it's not my signature.'

Before she knew what he was doing he'd reached across for a pen and paper. He stood up slightly and scrawled his name with his left hand, swung it round to her. 'I have a very distinctive signature because I'm left-handed.'

Maddie looked at it. It was completely different—and very much him. An arrogant scrawl. She knew deep down somewhere she didn't want to investigate that he wasn't lying. He was too proud, and he wouldn't hesitate to tell her that he had sent the letters if he had. Why would he lie? He hated her and wanted to see the back of her.

She forced down a disturbing emotion and looked at him. 'So, who sent them, then?'

'The early ones *are* from my father and his solicitor. But once he died someone started faking my signature. I think I know who it is but I'll confirm it for myself first, if you don't mind.'

Maddie nodded.

Nic reached out to take his cup, and swallowed the dark strong coffee in one gulp. 'I've taken up enough of your time.'

He stood up, and she rose to her feet as well. To her chagrin, her first response wasn't relief that he was going.

Maddie felt seriously unsettled and more than a little vulnerable as she acknowledged that he *hadn't* sent the letters. She followed him out and said carefully, 'So this means the pressure to force me to sell up will stop?'

Nic turned at the front door and smiled down at Maddie. But any hint of friendliness was gone. It was a cold and hard smile, and reminded her succintly of who she was dealing with. She took a step back.

'Nothing has changed really, Maddie. I still want you gone so I know we'll never have to deal with a Vasquez again. But there are other means of persuasion than letters. Much more pleasurable means.'

Maddie cursed her gullibility, and the way her belly had quivered when he'd said *pleasurable*. 'I said it once and I'll say it again. It'll be over my dead body, de Rojas. I'm not going anywhere.'

He shook his head. 'And we were doing so well—on first-name terms. Face the facts, Maddie. You need a massive injection of capital to make this vineyard lucrative again, and even then it would take years of good vintages to undo the damage that's been done. Your degree, while commendable, means nothing when you've got no wine or fertile vines to work with. You haven't even got electricity.'

Maddie smiled brilliantly, hiding her panic that she'd told him so much. 'We do have electricity, actually. I managed to pay some money into the account so we're not totally destitute. Now, if you're quite finished with your fact-finding mission, I'd appreciate it if you got lost.'

Maddie took great satisfaction in slamming the door in Nic's face, and only breathed out shakily when she heard his Jeep roaring away. She leant back against the front door and blew some hair out of her face.

Just then Maria appeared from the direction of the kitchen. 'We need more diesel for the generator. It's just died again.'

Maddie could have laughed if she wasn't afraid she'd start crying. She'd told a white lie about the electricity, determined not to let Nic de Rojas know she was so vulnerable. But the fact was that things were much, much worse than even he could ever know. She did need a massive injection of capital, and right now the only option open to her was to look for an investor.

She pushed herself off the front door. She knew exactly who she *wouldn't* be approaching for that help. She shivered slightly when she thought that his *other* methods of persuasion would have a lot to do with showing her just how much she hungered for him, and in the process gain some measure of vengeance for the way she'd rejected him eight years ago. And for the affair between her mother and his father which had wreaked such havoc.

Whatever his meaning, Maddie knew that if she allowed any kind of intimacy between them he would have the power to break her in two—and she could not allow him that satisfaction.

Nic's hands tightened on the steering wheel of his Jeep as he drove away. The knuckles showed white through his skin and he had to consciously relax. He didn't doubt that Maddie was lying about the electricity, and he didn't like the feeling that he was backing her into a corner where she felt she had to put up such a front.

Dammit. Nic slapped a hand on the steering wheel. It was only as he'd been walking out of her father's study that he'd realised the magnitude of what he was doing. He was the first in his family to come to the Vasquez estate and he had done it as unthinkingly as taking two steps forward…because he'd wanted to see her.

That need had transcended the paltry excuse to return her shoes, or to question her about her degree. As soon as he'd come within feet of her he'd wanted her so badly he'd been able to taste it on his tongue. He could remember her scent, and the way she'd tasted all those years before. Despite making sure his bed was a busy place in the meantime. Even if he was blindfolded he knew with grim certainty that he could pick Maddie out in a line-up. And he hadn't even slept with her. Yet.

Damn. He cursed her again. He'd seen the stubborness in every line of her body. He knew it well because it was deeply embedded in him too. A fierce drive to succeed and prevail.

Nic had been a sickly baby and child. His mother had suffered complications during the birth and hadn't been able to get pregnant again. His father had gone slowly mad with grief because the entire legacy of his family's estate rested on the shoulders of this one surviving weedy child.

And, even though Nic had become strong and healthy, his father had never seemed to be able to trust in Nic's ability completely. Nic's mouth twisted—not even when he'd achieved the remarkable feat of becoming a Master of Wine at the age of twenty-eight, when there was only a seven per cent success rate in graduating first time around.

Nic knew now that his childhood frailty had most likely had more to do with his mother's overprotectiveness than anything else, but from as far back as he could remember he'd known that he had to overcome the lethargy and allergies that held him back. And he had done it, slowly but surely, with single-minded determination and a deep desire to see his father look at him without that awful disappointment in his eyes.

By the time he was twelve he'd been bigger than most of the other boys in his class at school. His asthma had disappeared and his constitution had been as strong as an ox's. The doctor who'd used to come and see him had shaken his head and said, 'I've never seen anything like it in my life...'

Nic knew it was no miracle. It had been sheer determination to succeed. No one had ever known about that very dark and personal struggle to be strong and prevail. Until he'd told Maddie one day at the orchard. The words had slipped out of him before he'd even realised it, and even now he could see those huge green eyes, limpid with empathy, causing an ache in his heart.

Nic's hands tightened on the steering wheel again, hot anger coursing through him because he'd once been so gullible. Fooled by a pretty face and a lithe young body. That feeling of kinship...had he been so desperate that he'd conjured it up? The thought had always stung him. As a consequence he'd never let any woman close again;

the minute any lover tried to explore more personal avenues he cut them off.

His avowal to Maddie that he wanted to see her gone for good had far more to do with getting rid of his growing obsession with her than any need to extend the de Rojas empire. She was trouble and he knew it. He wanted her, and yet he knew he had to resist her for his own sanity. But, conversely, he knew that the only way to regain any sense of sanity was to have her on her back, beneath him, bucking against him and screaming for release.

By the time Nic got back to his own home he was seriously irritated. He decided to make the most of his mood and act on his resolve of last night to have a chat with his soon-to-be *ex*-solicitor about the letters. Anger whipped through him again at the thought of what he'd done in Nic's name.

Two days later, Maddie was weary all over. She felt as if she was fighting a losing battle as she drove the Jeep home from Villarosa with a pathetic amount of groceries to feed herself, Maria and Hernan. The petrol gauge was nearly on empty.

For a brief moment she thought how easy it would be just to give in…to call Nic up and say, *Fine—you've won.* She would get enough money from the sale of the estate to keep Maria and Hernan in comfort for the rest of their lives.

Maddie saw the outline of the estate in the distance and her throat grew tight. Despite being shut out of the workings of the vineyard her whole life by her father because she was a girl, she loved it. Ever since she was tiny she'd been fascinated by the whole process. She could remember being carried on her brother's skinny shoulders and reaching out reverently to touch the grapes, in awe of how these plump and bitter-tasting fruits could be transformed into complex and delicious wines.

Her blood sang here. She felt attuned to the earth and the seasons. Its backdrop of the magnificent snow-topped Andes was an image she'd held in her head during the long years of exile from her home. And now that she was back she wouldn't allow Nic de Rojas to run her off again just because he wanted to extend his empire.

But she faced an uphill battle. She'd just left the bank in Villarosa, where the manager had spent half an hour pointing out how impossible it was for him even to think about a business loan in the current economic climate.

The bank had been her last option. Over the past few days she'd gone to other vintners in the area, and one by one they'd all told her they weren't interested in investing. One of them had at least had the honesty to say, 'We simply can't go up against de Rojas. If he sees us investing in you it'll be like waving a red flag. He's too successful and we can't afford to get drawn into your feud…'

So even without lifting a finger Maddie was damned by her poisoned association with de Rojas. For ever.

When she saw his gleaming Jeep and his tall rangy body leaning against the bonnet with arms folded as she drove up to the house, her blood boiled over. She swung out of her Jeep and took out the shopping bags, holding them in front of her like a shield.

He made a movement to help and Maddie grabbed them tighter to her. 'I thought I told you you weren't welcome here.'

He had the gall to smile. 'Are you always so prickly in the evening? I must remember that for future reference. Perhaps you're a morning person.'

Maddie sensed him following her inside. She put down the bags on the nearest table and whirled around, hands on hips. Adrenalin was washing away her recent weariness. 'De Rojas, you're not welcome here. In fact I've heard your name enough in the past few days to last me a lifetime. So please, just *go*.'

Maddie would have physically pushed him, but was too afraid to touch him. Too afraid of her reaction when she could already feel it building up inside her. The insatiable need to drink him in, taste him. He was smartly dressed today, in chinos and a white shirt. Every inch the relaxed, successful vintner. She'd dressed smartly too, for the bank. She'd even splashed out with her fast-dwindling money to buy something that would fit, conscious of Nic's recent criticism.

As if reading her thoughts, he let that blue gaze drop and took in the pencil skirt, court shoes and tailored blouse. And then lazily he returned it all the way to where her hair was in a chignon.

'I like the office look—very demure.'

Maddie's hands became fists. She didn't feel demure. She felt hot. All over.

Before she could say anything else he said, 'Apparently you've been looking for an investor. I can tell by your mood you're not having much luck.'

Maddie choked back a curse and said, as calmly as she could, 'Unsurprisingly the local wine community don't want to upset their vastly more successful neighbour. How does it feel to know you're the don of the area, Nic? Does it make you feel powerful to know that people are too scared to invest because they might incur your wrath? That's hardly going to encourage healthy competition, now, is it? It's very easy to be successful in a vacuum.'

He flushed at that. 'Your father would be able to tell you all about that if he were still alive.' He elaborated. 'Your family was the first to quash any local competition, preferring to keep things simple and just between ourselves. If you'd done your research you'd know that more vintners have sprung up since the demise of your estate than ever before—and I've actually invested in some of them.'

Now Maddie flushed. Once again he was doing—or saying—the opposite of what she'd expected. She didn't like the way he was constantly putting her on the back foot.

His continued coolly. 'I came to tell you that my father's solicitor was responsible for the letters. He was a close friend of my father for many years and, unbeknownst to me, made a promise to him on his deathbed that he would continue to wage a campaign to get your father to sell. I suspect he also had a long-standing crush on my mother, and when she committed suicide he vowed some kind of vengeance on your father for having told her of the affair.'

Maddie sat down on a chair behind her. A sense of futility washed over her. Would the tangled mess that lay between them ever stop sending out poisonous tendrils into the future?

'Thank you for letting me know.' She looked up at Nic and saw something suspiciously like concern on his face, but it was quickly gone so she must have imagined it.

'I've also taken the liberty of paying your electricity bill for the forseeable future.'

Now Maddie sprang up, incensed. 'What did you do that for? I told you we were fine.'

Casually Nic reached out to a nearby switch and flicked it. Nothing happened, and Maddie went puce.

Just as casually he said, 'I knew you were lying. I'm doing it because it's a serious health and safety issue. I can't very well stand by and let an accident happen when I could have helped prevent it. Full power will be restored any time now.'

Feeling impotent with anger, Maddie quivered all over.

She couldn't say anything because when Hernan had gone out to get the generator going again he'd almost tripped and done himself a serious injury in the dark. Nic had her in a bind. How could she jeopardise the safety of her employees so wantonly by refusing this? And yet how could she accept?

'Like I said, Maddie, I just want you gone. I don't want you dead.' He arched a brow. 'Is it so hard to say, *Thank you, Nic*?'

Maddie's voice was constricted with the feeling of impotence, but finally she got out, 'What do you want from me?'

Nic came close to where Maddie stood and she fought not to let him see how she trembled when he got close. His eyes were all too assessing, and she could almost hear his brain whirring.

His jaw clenched, and then he said in a hard, flat voice, 'Dinner with me tonight. At my house.'

Maddie swallowed and fought the urge to run. He wasn't finished with pointing out how far she had to go to catch up. She longed to be able to say no, to refuse. But he had her in a corner, with no room to manoeuvre. The safety of her loyal staff was too important.

Ungraciously, she finally gritted out, 'Fine.'

After an infinitesimal moment when the very air around them seemed to vibrate with awareness and tension, he turned and walked out, leaving Maddie feeling as limp as a dishrag. She sank back onto the chair, her mind churning painfully.

He'd just pulled the rug from under her feet by doing an amazingly generous thing—and now, by asking her for dinner, he was blurring the lines, reinforcing the fact that he threatened her on many more levels than just the professional one.

Perhaps this was Nic's plan? To chip away at all the places where he would show up her weaknesses until he had her exactly where he wanted her. Maddie shivered when an image popped into her head of her lying back on a huge bed, with Nic looming over her like a marauding pirate. She would have to tell him tonight in no uncertain terms that she would repulse any further gesture, and set up a payment plan to pay him back for the electricity.

As if proving a point, suddenly the dark hallway was flooded with light. Maddie looked up and blinked, and then Maria rushed out from the kitchen, her eyes suspiciously bright. She came and hugged Maddie and said emotionally, 'Oh, *niña*, now I know everything will be all right...'

Maddie didn't have the heart to tell her that the sword of Damocles swung over them as much as it ever had.

'Good evening, Señorita Vasquez. Please come in.'

Maddie swallowed her nerves and stepped onto the flag-stoned floor of Nic's palatial hallway. Soft lights sent out a golden glow, reminding Maddie of how seductive it had been here the first time around. She tried to steel herself against it but it was hard.

She followed Geraldo through the now-empty court-yard, with its burbling fountain and flowers blooming out of pots everywhere, and into the main drawing room. He led her to a drinks cabinet and said solicitously, 'Señor de Rojas will join you shortly. He's been held up with a phone call. Please, can I offer you a drink?'

Maddie smiled tightly. 'Sparkling water would be fine.' She fully intended to keep her wits about her tonight.

Geraldo gave her the drink, and then excused himself after telling her to make herself comfortable. Maddie caught a glimpse of her reflection in a framed picture and smoothed down her skirt. It was the same one she'd been wearing earlier, but she'd teamed it with a dark grey silk top that thankfully was her own, and fitted. It was loose, with a wide neck, and she adjusted it now so that it wasn't falling down over one shoulder. She'd dithered over her hair and finally tied it up, not wanting Nic to think for a second that she was trying to seduce him.

She wandered over to a wall that was full of framed photos. She became more and more intrigued as she inspected what was obviously a history of the de Rojas family.

'Please forgive me for keeping you.'

Maddie's grip tightened on her glass before she turned around. Nic was standing in the doorway dressed in black pants and a pale blue shirt, open at the neck. His thick dark blond hair shone in the dim light, and those blue eyes took her breath away even now.

Maddie suddenly felt inexplicably shy, and it unnerved her. She'd had to develop a thick skin to survive these past few years and she didn't like this new vulnerability that Nic de Rojas seemed to bring out in her with such effortless ease. 'It's fine. I wasn't waiting long.'

He came towards her then, and stopped near the photos. He gestured with his head and Maddie had to tear her eyes off him. 'My family—all the way back to the nineteenth century, before they left Spain to come here.'

Maddie found herself smiling slightly. 'We have a wall like this too. I always wonder why my ancestors looked so fierce in the pictures.'

'Times were hard then…they had to fight to survive.'

Maddie snuck a glance at Nic. Something about the way he'd said that caught at her insides. At that moment she had a vivid memory of him revealing to her once how sickly he'd been as a child, and how hard he'd struggled to overcome that physical frailty. He was so virile now, so *vital*, that it was almost impossible to believe.

Then he was stepping back and the moment was gone. He indicated with a hand for her to precede him. 'Let me show you into the dining room.'

Maddie moved forward jerkily. She cursed Nic for making her remember things and for putting on this chivalrous act. It was so much easier to deal with him when the lines of battle were clearly drawn.

Nic solicitously pulled out her chair for her, and waited till she'd sat down before taking his own seat opposite. It was a small, intimate table, with candles flickering and lending a far too seductive air for Maddie's liking.

'An aperitif to whet the palate?'

Maddie looked up and fought the urge to adjust her top and let some air get to her skin. She was suddenly boiling. He was weaving some sort of sensual spell over her. And she hated to admit it but she was curious to know about the wines Nic would choose. She was having dinner with a Master of Wine, after all. There were only a few hundred in the world—a very select group.

'Just a small amount. I'm driving.'

He inclined his head and dutifully poured a taster into her glass from a bottle whose label was obscured. It was a white wine. Maddie lifted it and let the clear liquid swirl for a moment before dipping her head and breathing deep. As soon as the bouquet registered she paled dramatically. Nic watched her carefully.

Maddie didn't taste the wine and put the glass down with a trembling hand. She looked at him, willing down an incredible surge of emotion. 'Is this some kind of a joke?'

CHAPTER FIVE

Nic was innocence personified. 'Why would it be a joke?'

Maddie was vibrating with tension now. 'You serve me a Vasquez wine—why? Are you expecting me not to recognise it? Is this a test?'

Maddie put down her napkin and stood up, a little bewildered at how emotional she was feeling, afraid that it was coming partly from that memory just moments ago.

Nic's hand snaked out and caught her wrist. 'Sit down. Please.' When she just looked at him and tried to pull her wrist out of his grip he smiled ruefully. 'I'll admit that I was curious as to whether or not you would know the wine.'

Maddie pulled her wrist free finally but didn't sit down. She looked down at Nic with her most haughty expression. 'Of course I recognise the wine. I grew up watching those very grapes ripen every year.'

Passion made her voice low and fervent. Maddie sat down abruptly—conflicted about how she was feeling. So Nic had served her a Vasquez wine? What was the big deal?

As if reading her mind, he frowned at her now. 'I didn't mean to anger you.'

'No,' snapped Maddie. 'You were just testing me, to

see if I really know my stuff or if I slept my way to getting my degree, is that it?'

Now Nic flushed dark red. 'I don't believe you manipulated your results.'

To Maddie's chagrin, hot tears burnt the back of her eyes and she blinked furiously, only vaguely satisfied when she saw Nic's horrorstruck face. She knew the emotion was coming from a complex mix of bittersweet grief for her father and the overwhelming pressure she was under— not to mention the passion Nic was able to evoke in her so effortlessly.

Exerting a valiant effort to bring herself under control, Maddie picked up the glass again and took a sip. She closed her eyes for a moment, letting the liquid rest in her mouth before slipping down her throat like smooth silk. She opened her eyes again and narrowed a fiery green gaze on Nic. 'If I'm not mistaken this is from the ninety-nine vintage. It won us the Prix de Vin for the best white in New World Wines that year.'

Nic inclined his head, his eyes focused on hers with unnerving intensity. 'You're right. My father bought a case of every vintage of Vasquez wines to analyse them. Exactly as your father did with our wines, I'm sure.'

Maddie nodded, and could feel some equilibrium returning. She looked away for a moment, and then back. 'I'm sorry...it just caught me unawares. That particular wine was always a favourite of mine.' Her voice was husky. 'It reminds me of home. *Here.*' Maddie's fingers pleated the napkin on the table. 'It always made me so homesick whenever I smelt it abroad. People used to order it in the restaurant where I worked, and I would pretend not to know that I should open it at the table just so I could open it first and smell it without anyone watching.'

She looked at Nic, and down again quickly when she saw that gaze, no less intense.

'It used to amaze me to think of this bottle coming all the way from our estate. It made me wonder about the year—had the seasons been kind to the grape? I could always tell just from the smell if it had been good or bad. I can't believe I never got fired for making such a *faux pas*, but the customers always seemed to forgive me.'

Nic watched as candlelight played over Maddie's pale skin, casting her features into mysterious shadows. Her cheekbones stood out. Her lips looked ripe and full. The grey silk of her top lay against her collarbone like the most decadent covering, and the swell of her breasts pushed enticingly against the slippery fabric. He could well imagine the customers forgiving her anything.

He'd never seen anything so sensuous as the way she was cradling her glass. He was transfixed by her natural beauty and her innate earthy sexiness, and all of a sudden he felt as if he was hurtling back in time and out of his depth. The terrain he'd been so sure of was shifting. She was articulating exactly how he felt about the wines he cultivated—each year the vintage *did have* a certain personality, a complexity.

Maddie was about to take another sip when she looked up to see Nic's mesmerised expression. She halted the glass before it got to her mouth. 'What is it?'

He shook his head and colour flared along his cheekbones, making Maddie feel off balance.

'Nothing. I shouldn't have tested you like that.' His mouth quirked in a wry smile. 'You seem to bring out the worst in me.'

Maddie had to fight down a burgeoning sense of lightness. 'I'll take that as a compliment.'

He lifted his glass to hers. *'Salud,'* he said, and then took a deep sip.

The sheer masculinity of his movements while doing something that was inherently delicate made Maddie's toes curl. He was such a *man.*

Much to her relief, their starter was served and eaten largely in silence, with Maddie berating herself for having come over all hysterical just because Nic had fancied giving her some sort of test. And for waxing lyrical about feeling homseick. As if Nic was at all interested in what she thought.

When the main course was served she focused on the meat with single-minded determination, savouring every succulent morsel.

Much to her surprise, they managed to conduct a civil conversation about neutral topics, and when Nic handed her a glass of red Maddie took it without a conscious awareness of how comfortable she'd become.

He said, 'Try this. It's a new blend I'm working on, and this is the first run of wine. I'm not marketing it yet.'

Maddie put down her fork. 'Are you sure you want to be sharing secrets with the enemy?'

Nic's mouth quirked. 'After seeing your vineyard I know I'm in no imminent danger.'

Maddie flushed at being reminded of the painful reality. She raised the glass to her mouth and forced herself to hold Nic's gaze, refusing to be the first to look away. But in the end she had to, because as she savoured the wine she closed her eyes instinctively to try and figure out the various components.

She opened them again and saw Nic watching her. It set a slow fire burning deep inside. Slowly she said, 'Well, it's a classic Malbec...but not like anything I've tasted before—it's got a strain of something else.'

Nic inclined his head. 'Very impressive.'

Maddie had to admit grudgingly, 'I like it. It's not as straightforward as the usual Malbecs—it's got more complexity…a dark side… Pinot?'

Nic smiled. 'I can see how you got your First.'

Maddie felt a ridiculous rush of pleasure go through her just as the attentive staff member came in and took their plates away.

Nic stood up and indicated for Maddie to precede him out of the open French doors to the patio outside. Her belly clenched for a moment—this was where he'd kissed her the other night. Then she saw that a smaller table for two had been set there, with more candles flickering in the breeze.

She almost wanted to back away and insist on leaving. But she was loath to give Nic the satisfaction of knowing that he was getting to her. She moved forward and sat down in the chair that Nic pulled out. Presently the waiter came back and served them both small dishes that held exquisite-looking lemon tart desserts. Nic opened a bottle of dessert wine and poured some for Maddie. Her mouth was already watering at the thought of the tart lemon soothed by the sweet wine.

Feeling churlish at how easily he was entrancing her, she said, 'You really don't have to do this, you know. It's not working.'

Nic smiled urbanely. 'What's not working? You've proved your point, Maddie. You're happier to live in squalor than to come running to me for home comforts. Clearly I underestimated your ability to put up with discomfort.'

Maddie's appetite disappeared and she said tightly, 'You underestimate a lot more than that, Nic. You don't know one thing about what happened when I left here. You seem to have this halcyon fantasy that I went to Europe and spent my time skiing and partying.'

Carefully he said, 'Why don't you tell me what you did?'

Maddie wanted to refuse, to tell him it was none of his business, but she had a desire to make him understand that she was made of sterner stuff, that she wouldn't just turn around and give up. And also a dangerous desire to see him regard her with something besides mockery or disbelief in his eyes...

'When my mother and I left here we left with nothing. My father threw us out and turned his back on us completely.' Her mouth tightened. 'We spent three years in Buenos Aires living with my aunt, who eventually threw us out. In the meantime Mother had been divorced and found herself a rich suitor. She gave me a one-way ticket to London to get me out of her hair.'

Maddie didn't want to elaborate and tell him that her mother had blamed Maddie for being left with nothing in the divorce. Her gaze remained resolutely forward, out into the darkness that encompassed his vast estate.

'I got to London and found work in a restaurant by night, and as a hotel chambermaid by day. The night you saw me in that club was pure chance. I'd never been in it before, or since then.' Maddie blushed when she thought of the picture she'd presented in the revealing dress. She rushed on. 'When I'd made enough money I moved to France and looked for work picking grapes for the summer. I ended up at the vineyard in Bordeaux, where Pierre Vacheron took me in.'

Maddie sent Nic a quick defensive look. 'He found out where I came from, that I had some knowledge of wine, and decided to give me one of the scholarships. I'd most likely still be there if my father hadn't written and asked me to come home. Pierre offered me a full-time job.'

Nic's face was expressionless. 'That magazine article painted a very different picture.'

Considering that since she had divulged so much already she might as well tell him the whole truth, Maddie laid out the bones of the painful reality of her relationship with her flighty and self-absorbed mother. The humiliation of the whole episode was vivid again.

When she'd finished she put down her dessert wine glass and stood up. The full enormity of her naivety was hitting her—to allow herself to think for a second that Nic de Rojas was as urbane and charming as he appeared this evening. With any other woman, yes. With her, *no.* He was just trying to unbalance her, and she was letting him.

'I want you to realise that I won't be easily dissuaded, or seduced by the trappings of wealth.'

Driven by the wave of ambiguous anger he was feeling, Nic said, 'Don't underestimate *my* determination to succeed in this matter, Maddie. I've proved how determined I can be over and over again.'

Maddie fought not to let Nic see how he was affecting her. 'So we're back where we started?'

Nic's gaze grew hot and moved to her mouth.

Maddie moved back, putting up a hand as if to ward him off. *'No...'*

He reached for her easily and pulled her into him. '*Yes.* This is where we started—and where we've yet to finish.'

And he bent his head and took her mouth in a kiss so incendiary and devastating that Maddie had no defence. Especially not after laying herself bare like that. Her hands clung onto his powerful biceps, her whole body arched into his—he was bending her back further and further with the sheer force of his kiss.

Lips ground into teeth which clashed and nipped at soft skin. Maddie tasted blood at one point and didn't know if it was hers or his. Their tongues duelled madly, in a hot

swirl. She only wanted *this*. She would have given everything up in that moment to prolong it…

And then abruptly Nic put her away from him with both
hands. 'Get out of here, Maddie.'

Maddie looked up, shocked, hurt and bewildered. Her
chest was aching with the effort to draw breath. She saw
the blood on his lip. She'd bitten him.

A need to claw back some control forced her to say
shakily, 'With pleasure. I won't whore myself to you for
my vineyard, Nic—the sooner you realise that the better.'

Nic stood in a haze of sexually frustrated agony for long
moments. On one level he couldn't fathom how he'd just
let Maddie go, but then he remembered the way she'd
kissed him back, biting his lip in her ardour. And *that*—
hot on the heels of her further revelations about her life
these past few years—had made him feel unaccountably
vulnerable.

He'd assumed Maddie and her mother had been given
plenty of money. He'd had no idea that her father had turfed
them out with no support, or that her mother had all but
turned her back on her too. That she'd had to take two me-
nial jobs just to survive.

Nic went over to the wooden perimeter on the decking
which wrapped around this side of the house. His hands
curled around it tightly and he took a deep breath, still
struggling for control. Kissing Maddie just now had reminded him too vividly of losing himself to her seductive
wiles before.

She'd spent a week reeling him in, making him trust
her with pathetic ease. Only to reveal in the end how she'd
really felt about seducing him. It had made her physically
ill. He'd watched the way she'd retched and coughed after
he'd touched her. Nic's stomach clenched hard. She must

have been very bored indeed to have pushed the limits of what she could endure for the sake of doing something exciting and illicit.

Something very private and vulnerable in him had been destroyed that day. He'd become hardened. Impenetrable. No woman since then had managed to crack his protective veneer, or challenge his cynicism. But the way Maddie had kissed him just now, and the way she'd kissed him the other night—as artlessly and yet as devastatingly as he remembered—was a threat for which he hadn't been prepared.

He'd thought he could handle kissing her, but tasting her again was dangerous—he felt himself slipping and sliding away from everything that held him rooted to reality and sanity.

Nic had developed a mild aversion to being touched after his mother's nervous and overprotective constant fussing, which had been in stark contrast to his father's habitual rages, when he'd used his fists freely. But when Maddie touched him, he couldn't get enough. It galled him now that he found every woman's touch invariably cloying or too possessive, but not *hers*. It made him very nervous to acknowledge that…which was why he'd pushed her back.

Something inside Nic hardened. He *would* have her—but on his terms. He would force her to be honest with him and herself. There would be no drama, regrets or recriminations this time. Only satisfaction and closure.

A couple of days later Maddie was sitting in her father's study and looking at another invitation. It was addressed to her father, and it was for the Annual South American Vintners' Gala Ball in two days' time. It was in a different city each year, and this year, as luck would have it, it was to be in Buenos Aires. So near—but so far.

Maddie sighed. Something like this was just what she

needed—a chance to meet people who only remembered Vasquez as a successful estate. It was the perfect place to look for investors. But she had no hope of flying to Buenos Aires where the ball was being held. She had no money for the flight, and anyway there was a national airline strike.

Just then the phone rang, and Maddie picked it up. She flushed all over when she heard an all-too-familiar deep voice on the other end. Then she felt cold when she remembered the way he'd aborted their kiss and pushed her from him the other night. She hated Nic de Rojas for exposing her weakness and desire like that. For rejecting her.

'Yes?' Her voice was as cold as she felt.

'Did you get your invitation?'

Maddie couldn't help her stubborn streak from rising up. 'What invitation?'

'You're such a terrible liar, Vasquez. I know you're probably looking at it right now and figuring out how to get there so you can sucker some poor investor into taking on your dead-end estate.'

Maddie made a face at the phone, and then said airily, 'Oh, you mean *that* invitation? Yes, I have it…why?'

'Are you going?'

Something in his voice made Maddie's hackles rise. 'Of course I'm going. Why wouldn't I?'

'No need to sound so defensive, Maddie—I was asking because I'm taking a private jet and was going to offer you a lift.'

Maddie's jaw dropped, but she quickly recovered. After the other night she wouldn't accept anything from this man. 'No, thank you.' She injected saccharine-sweetness into her voice. 'I've got alternative arrangements made. I'll see you there.'

She barely heard him mutter something about *'stub-*

born woman' before she cut him off. Maddie's heart was thumping. She'd have to go now. She couldn't afford to show Nicolás any weakness.

By the time Maddie arrived in Buenos Aires, sticky and hot, almost two days later, she ached all over. She'd taken a ridiculously long bus journey from Mendoza, and every bump in the road seemed to be engraved on her nerves.

Maddie hauled her bag behind her and joined the masses of people all making their way to various destinations. Hers was the cheapest hotel she'd been able to find close to the Grand Palace Buenos Aires hotel, where the gala was due to take place that evening.

When she finally found her room and looked at herself in the mirror, she realised that she had a mountain of work to do to make herself look every inch the successful vintner she wanted to portray herself as being.

Nic didn't like the sense of anticipation firing up his blood. This fizzing expectancy. He was used to being in control at all times, and right now he felt off-kilter. He realised that it was because he didn't know where *she* was. He'd almost gone to her home and forced her to come with him on his plane, but a sensation of lingering rawness after the other night had stopped him.

And how the hell had she even got here? He knew it couldn't have been by air because of the strike, which was why he'd ordered the private jet.

Just then he spotted a familiar face in the crowd and he smiled warmly, welcoming the distraction.

Maddie's stomach was in knots. She took a deep breath and stepped into the thronged ballroom. She'd managed to ferret out another of her mother's dresses, and mercifully this one fitted. It was green and shimmery, it fell to the floor, and it was relatively demure, with long sleeves and a high neck. But when she walked one pale leg was exposed, thanks to a thigh-high slit. Maddie had cursed when she'd discovered it; the sooner she could afford to supplement her own wardrobe again, the better.

She'd used her practically maxed-out credit card to buy some cheap shoes and get her hair done in a salon, and now it lay in lustrous-looking waves over one shoulder. She was glad she'd spent the money when she saw how immaculate everyone else looked. She just hoped they wouldn't notice that her emerald earrings had come from a costume-jewellery shop.

And then she saw Nic across the room. Her hands tightened reflexively on the clutch bag she carried in front of her like a shield. She hated the awful feeling of excitement that danced along her veins at seeing him again. He wasn't looking at her, though; he was looking down at the woman in front of him and smiling in a way that made an awful yearning go through Maddie.

And then, to her horror, as if they were connected by some telepathic thread of awareness, he looked up and straight at her. His smile faded. The woman he'd been talking to looked over as well, and Maddie felt her belly hollow out when she recognised the same stunning blonde from the first night she'd seen him again in Mendoza.

Someone came by with a tray full of champagne and Maddie grabbed a glass inelegantly because she could see Nic taking his companion by the hand and leading her towards Maddie. It was as if she was rooted to the spot. She couldn't move, and with everything in her head and heart she cursed him—because he was going to introduce her to his mistress and make her feel like dirt.

He came closer and closer, a curiously intent look on

his face and in his eyes. Maddie was stuck like a deer in the headlights. She'd never felt so alone or exposed. She should never have come…she should have known he'd take any opportunity to humiliate her…

'Maddie, you made it…I'll resist the temptation to ask how you did it.'

Maddie's voice wouldn't work for a long moment. She could feel a curious glance from the stunning blonde, and hot, angry colour seeped into her cheeks. She'd never been in this situation before—having kissed another woman's man. And she was disappointed. Somehow she hadn't expected this kind of behaviour from him.

'…like you to meet someone.'

Like watching a car crash in slow motion, Maddie managed to look at the other woman and smile, but it felt numb. She realised then that the woman was much younger than Maddie had realised—about twenty at the most. Now she felt sick—and also, more worryingly, as if she wanted to gouge her eyes out.

'This is my cousin Estella. You would have met her at the wine-tasting evening, but she had to be in BA for a modelling assignment. She's in high demand. Not to mention that she breaks out in hives after a couple of days in the country.'

The girl looked adoringly at Nic and hit him playfully on his shoulder. 'Hardly hives, Nic. You do like to exaggerate, don't you?'

Maddie was aware that the girl was exquisite, beautiful, and had a sense of humour. And then it sank in properly. *My cousin.*

Maddie forced her throat to work, and tried to ignore the relief flooding her. 'It's nice to meet you, Estella,' she said scratchily.

'You too, Maddie.' She turned her sunny smile back to Nic and said, 'I'd better go and find my date or he'll be sending out a search party.'

'I need to meet this man who is going to pretend that he *won't* be sharing your hotel room tonight.'

Maddie looked at Nic and saw an endearingly stern look on his face. His cousin blushed, but rolled her eyes. 'Yes, Nic, but please don't give him the third degree. He's a nice guy, really.'

She jumped up and pressed a kiss to Nic's cheek, then was gone with a flash of blonde hair and sinuous tanned limbs.

Maddie was mesmerised by Nic's fond gaze after his cousin, so she wasn't prepared when he turned to look at her and his whole visage became noticeably cooler.

'I booked her a room for the night because I don't like her going back out to the suburbs too late. At least this way I know she's safe. Her father was my mother's brother. He died when she was small, so I've become a sort of…father figure for her.'

Maddie's belly clenched at hearing how protective Nic was of his cousin. A bit redundantly she said, 'She seems nice.'

Someone bumped into Maddie at that moment, and she winced. She could feel that she had a bruise on one hip.

'What is it?'

The sudden urgency in Nic's voice made her look up. 'Nothing. I'm just a bit sore after—' She stopped herself there. But it wasn't long before a dawning realistion came into Nic's eyes.

'You took the bus, didn't you?' He shook his head. 'Of all the stubborn—' He stopped and cursed. 'How long was it? Fourteen hours?'

Maddie cursed him, and then admitted painfully, 'Sixteen, actually. We got a flat tyre.'

He shook his head at her and then said, 'I suppose you're here to look for an investor?'

Maddie flushed. 'What other choice do I have? It's find an investor or lose everything to you.'

'You'd be a very wealthy woman.'

Something painful twisted in Maddie's chest at hearing him reiterate that he wanted her gone at all costs. It made her feel very nervous and she lashed out. 'Why can't you get it through that thick skull of yours that it's not about the money? I love my estate and I want to restore it to its full potential.'

Nic's jaw clenched. He opened his mouth, but just then the gong sounded for the gala dinner. Maddie took the opportunity to flee in the ensuing crush, grateful that she didn't feel a strong hand on her arm. She had every intention of talking to as many people as possible and staying away from one person in particular.

All during dinner Nic was aware of Maddie across the other side of the table. She was seated beside Alex Morales, one of the most successful vintners in the US—a man Nic had never particularly liked or trusted without ever having analysed why. It was a gut reaction, and it was becoming stronger by the second.

He couldn't concentrate on the conversations either side of him and he wanted to snarl at the pouting redhead across the table who seemed determined to give him a bird's-eye view of her surgically enhanced cleavage.

All Nic could imagine was Maddie's huge green eyes imploring Morales to invest in her poor vineyard, and he had to physically restrain himself from walking over, plucking her from the chair and carrying her far away.

Maddie looked at her attentive and charming dinner companion incredulously. 'You'd really like to discuss this further?'

The man smiled and oozed charm. 'Of course, my dear.'

He was a little cheesy for Maddie's liking, but she wasn't about to dismiss a potential investor because of a possibly erroneous gut feeling.

She couldn't believe she'd had the good fortune to be seated next to Alex Morales, and that he was interested in learning more about the Vasquez estate. This could be the solution to all her problems. If she could persuade Morales to invest in her she'd be free of Nic's influence.

Maddie had been uncomfortably aware of Nic's gaze on her all throughout the dinner but she'd done her best to ignore him. However, with this exciting development, she couldn't help glancing over in his direction. She hated that she met that blue gaze so effortlessly, as if drawn by a magnet. He was looking impossibly grim. She smiled and his eyes flashed. Maddie knew it was childish, but she was buoyed up to think that her problems could soon be over.

People were already getting up and moving out to the ballroom, which had been cleared for dancing with tables set around the dance floor. Morales took Maddie's hand to guide her from her seat. His touch lingered a little too long for Maddie's liking, but she quashed the flutter of doubt, telling herself she had to explore this opportunity.

He bowed slightly in a disarmingly old-fashioned gesture. 'If you'd excuse me? I have an important call I have to make, but I will be available in about thirty minutes if you'd like to continue our discussion?'

Maddie's eagerness was dismayingly obvious. 'I really appreciate this, Mr Morales.'

'Please...' He smiled, showing glaringly white teeth. 'Call me Alex. Why don't you meet me at my room—say in thirty-five minutes?'

He told her his room number and was turning away when sudden panic gripped Maddie. Their conversation had just taken a turn she really hadn't expected.

She reached for Morales's arm and he turned back, one eyebrow raised. 'Yes?'

Immediately Maddie felt gauche. 'I'm sorry, but... wouldn't it be easier to meet in one of the bars?'

Morales smiled, and it was faintly patronising. 'I have to make the call in my room, so it really would be easier if you came to me. All of the bars will be full and very loud. Of course, if this discussion isn't that important to you...'

His voice trailed off and Maddie picked up his meaning instantly, seeing her chance floating away.

'No, no,' she said hurriedly, telling herself that he sounded reasonable. 'Your room will be fine. Absolutely fine.'

He inclined his head and then walked away. Only to be replaced almost immediately by someone taller and far more disturbing. Maddie tried to walk around Nic but he blocked her.

She glared up at him. 'Yes?'

Nic's jaw was tense and his eyes were flashing. 'I don't trust that man.'

CHAPTER SIX

'OH, please,' Maddie sneered. 'You just can't bear the thought that someone else might see the potential in my estate and want to invest in me.'

Nic's eyes flashed. 'I think he wants to invest, all right, but it's not necessarily in your estate. Where are you meeting him?'

Maddie went puce. She refused to answer and went to walk around Nic again, but he caught her arm in a big hand. Maddie gritted her teeth against the instant chemical reaction in her body.

He was incredulous. 'Don't tell me you're going to meet him in his room? Is that what that little conference was about?' Maddie went even more red and Nic exploded, 'For crying out loud, Maddie, you're too inexperienced to deal with someone like Morales. He'll chew you up and spit you out!'

Maddie reacted viscerally. Little did Nic know how inexperienced she really was—physically *and* in situations like these. But every ounce of pride demanded that she project an image of confidence. She looked up at Nic and tossed her hair back. She smiled up at him and hoped it had the same slightly patronising edge that Morales had just used on her.

'Do you really think I haven't met men like Morales before now? I know his type, Nic. He just needs to be played a certain way.'

Nic's face flushed and he dropped her arm suddenly, as if it was poisonous. Immediately Maddie felt bereft.

He sounded utterly disgusted. 'Forgive me for thinking for a second that you might be going into a situation you're not equipped to handle. If he's the kind of investor you want, and you're willing to do what it takes, then clearly I've underestimated you *and* your ambition.'

Nic took a step back from her and walked away, leaving Maddie feeling vulnerable and insecure. What exactly had Nic meant by not trusting Morales? She recalled his smooth smile and shuddered a little. Surely even if he came on to her she could just walk away?

Maddie didn't like the way Nic had made her feel slightly ashamed just now, or the feeling, for a brief moment, that he might be concerned for her safety. Maddie wasn't used to anyone else stepping in to fight her battles for her. Her brother had been the only one who'd ever stood up for her, and he'd died a long time ago.

Realising that she was standing and brooding in an empty dining room, Maddie knew she had to move. She glanced at her watch and cursed silently. It was already nearly time to meet Morales. Pushing down the sudden trepidation she felt, Maddie hurried to the lifts.

Nic was standing in one of the hotel bars with some acquaintances when he saw a flash of green out of the corner of his eye and looked to see Maddie disappear into a lift. His stomach clenched so hard for a second that his vision blurred slightly. He couldn't believe that she was actually going through with it. He'd underestimated her, all right. Underestimated her greed and her ambition to succeed no matter what it took.

Nic battled for a long moment with the seething emotions in his gut and then one overriding feeling rose up as he recalled Maddie's defiance just now, and her flushed face. Surely she wasn't doing this to get at *him*?

Nic put down his glass and excused himself. In hindsight, and when she wasn't standing in front of him and scrambling his brain cells with her proximity, her bravado seemed far too brittle.

He quickly got Morales's room number and strode to the lifts, punching the button. And then something stopped him—maybe he had completely misread the way she'd kissed him with such artless fervour? Maybe she changed her method for each man and gave them what she thought they wanted? Maybe she was playing Nic—kissing him the way she suspected would affect him most, reminding him of those gauche responses in the orchard that day?

The lift doors opened and Nic was torn. He couldn't move. Was he really going to go after Maddie and risk exposing himself all over again? He could already see her mocking face when she opened Morales's door. What the hell was he going to say when he *did* get up to the room?

'Nic! There you are. I've been looking for you everywhere. You have to come and meet Louis...he's waiting for you.'

Nic looked down at his cousin, who had just hooked her arm into his, and felt slightly dazed. Suddenly everything came back into perspective and he cursed this bout of uncharacteristic indecision. He felt nothing for Maddie except mistrust and antipathy—along with an annoying level of desire. Estella was someone he loved unconditionally. Who was more important to him?

He smiled down at her and said, 'Lead the way.' And as Estella dragged him in her wake Nic pushed aside all thoughts of the sable-haired witch, telling himself that Maddie was certainly able to handle herself.

He ignored the slightly ominous sound of the lift doors closing again behind him.

Maddie was stuck in a waking nightmare. She had locked herself inside the bathroom in Morales's suite and was shaking all over. She had no idea how much time had passed. But mercifully he'd stopped thumping on the bathroom door and calling her names a few minutes ago.

Carefully she stood up and went over to the sink. She looked at herself in the mirror. Her eyes widened in shock—her hair was a mess, her dress was torn at the neck and blood was oozing from a cut lip. She was still in shock. She couldn't really believe what had happened.

Her first indication that something was wrong should have been the fact that he was obviously more inebriated than he had been downstairs. But at first Morales had been charming. And interested. He'd disarmed her and made her feel as if she was overreacting. She'd tried to ignore the fact that his words were slurring slightly and that he was a little unsteady on his feet.

She'd launched into her spiel about the estate. But then he'd come over to sit beside her and put his hand high on her thigh. Immediately panicked, Maddie had jerked back, dislodging his hand. Everything had changed in an instant. He'd turned into a monster.

In the struggle that had ensued he'd ripped her dress and slapped her across the face. Maddie had somehow managed to push him off her and made for the only route of escape or safety she could see. She had locked herself in the bathroom. Morales had shouted obscenities, and she'd been terrified he'd break the door down. But now, after long minutes, everything was mercifully quiet.

Maddie crept over to the door and listened. Her heart leapt when she heard the unmistakable sound of snoring. With her pulse beating fast, she turned the lock silently and opened the door, half terrified it would smash open in her face.

She saw Morales sprawled on the couch, fast asleep with his mouth open wide. Nearly crying with relief, Maddie crept out—all the way to the main door. Her hands were shaking so badly she almost couldn't open it, and when it did open she all but fell into the corridor. She only realised then that her shoes had come off somewhere along the way in the struggle, but there was no way she would go back and get them now.

Forcing herself to keep moving, she set off to find the lift.

Nic rounded a corner in the corridor where he'd walked Estella back to her room, much to her amusement, and stopped dead when he saw a familiar figure walking towards him. Recognition was like a hot poker in his belly. He knew this was Morales's floor, and hadn't liked to admit that part of his motivation in walking Estella to her room had been for that reason. Had he really been hoping to bump into Maddie making her walk of shame? Well, his subconscious desire had manifested her right in front of him.

Anger rose like a swift tide of lava inside him. And something else much more potent and disturbing. *Jealousy.* An alien emotion because no other woman had ever aroused it in him.

In that moment Maddie looked up and saw him. She stopped dead and froze like a deer in the headlights. Nic heard something inarticulate like a sob coming from her throat, and then she turned and was walking back the way she'd come. Away from him.

All Nic was aware of was her *déshabillé* and mussed-up hair. And then he saw her bare feet. His anger became white-hot. Being barefoot made her look ridiculously vulnerable, but she'd just been— Bile rose in Nic's throat, and before he even knew what he was doing he was pursuing her, driven by dark and angry demons.

When he was close enough to reach out and touch her he stopped, and said with scorn dripping from every word, 'Well? Did you give Morales everything he wanted or just enough of a taste to keep him interested?' Disgust and something else—*disappointment*—lanced Nic in a very vulnerable place.

Maddie stopped too, her shoulders a tense line. She didn't turn around. 'Just leave me alone, Nic.'

Her voice sounded husky and raw, and it made Nic even angrier. She was still playing on his emotions. He reached for her shoulder and swung her round—but when he saw her face the bottom fell out of his stomach.

Instinctively he put his other hand on her other shoulder. 'Maddie…what the hell…? Did Morales do this?'

Maddie tried to look away, or down, but Nic gently tipped her chin up so he could inspect her face. He cursed volubly. Maddie jerked her chin out of his hold and pulled back. The blood on her split lip looked garish against the stark paleness of her face.

'What, Nic? Aren't you going to say I told you so? You did warn me, after all, not to trust him.'

Maddie was struggling to hold it together, to be strong. She couldn't bear it that Nic was witness to her awful humiliation. She'd never felt so frail or weak. Or useless. And she hated the lingering terror that made her want to cling onto his solid strength. She looked down, tears suddenly stinging her eyes.

He sounded tortured. 'When I said I didn't trust Morales, it was a gut instinct. I've never liked him, or his business methods, but I had no idea he was capable of violence.'

Maddie was bitter. 'Well, it would seem your instincts have been proved right.'

He asked then, 'When did he do this to you? After...?'

Maddie looked up at Nic in abject horror, forgetting about her tears. He thought that she'd *slept* with Morales anyway? How low was his opinion of her? Bile rose and she was afraid she'd be sick. And yet who did she have to blame but herself when she'd been so intent on proving to Nic that she was *experienced*?

Suddenly the fight left Maddie. The shock that had been numbing her wore off. The awful shaking that hadn't abated. It seemed to intensify all over her body. 'I didn't sleep with him. That was never my intention.' She shuddered reflexively. 'I couldn't...with a man like that...just to get something. You can call me naive, or whatever you want, but I went to his room believing that we would just talk about business.'

Maddie took a deep shaky breath, and avoided Nic's eye again. 'But then...he was all over me...and I couldn't move or breathe. He'd been drinking. I hadn't realised how much. He ripped my dress and then he slapped me...'

To Maddie's horror she started crying in earnest, great deep racking sobs that seemed to come out of nowhere and she couldn't control them. She felt so cold. Suddenly heat engulfed her and she felt herself being drawn into an embrace of solid muscle. Musky male scent surrounded her. And finally she felt safe. Unbelievably safe.

Maddie was incredibly slender and vulnerable in Nic's

arms, her slim body trembling violently. The protective instinct was almost overwhelming. He wanted to believe her so badly he could taste it.

To see her crushed like this was almost as hard as if she'd been defiant and triumphant. No one could fake the terror he could feel in her body. Nic's vision was red. His father had used to hit his mother whenever she angered him, and Nic had an absolute abhorrence of violence against women. The rage he felt towards Morales scared him with its intensity.

Yet he found it hard to believe that Maddie hadn't known what she was walking into by agreeing to meet him in his room. How could she have been so naive? An experienced woman like her? Had she just been playing out of her league? Not counting on Morales turning violent?

Deep inside Nic was shame and self-recrimination that he'd allowed Maddie to walk into that situation. That he'd let his own pride stop him from following his initial gut instinct to go after her. This woman had him so tied up in knots that he'd prefer to let her be in danger than deal with her. He was pathetic.

Nic held Maddie for a long time, until her sobs had stopped. His hands moved up and down her back, soothing her. *Déjà vu* hit him straight in his belly when he remembered another time and place, when he'd held this woman in his arms after seeing her in tears. He tensed against the inevitable pain that accompanied those memories, but for the first time it didn't come.

She'd stopped shaking and crying, and was as still as a mouse in his arms. He could feel her breath, warm through the flimsy material of his shirt. And just like that the protective instinct was dissolving in a rush of heat and arousal. Her body was moulding against his as if made for him alone. Every curve fitted perfectly into his harder planes.

Nic gritted his jaw, but he couldn't stop his body responding to her proximity, or the way it felt to have her soft breasts crushed against his chest.

When she tensed slightly and shifted, Nic loosened his hold.

Maddie realised that she'd just fallen into Nic's arms like some kind of wilting heroine and felt embarrassed. She pulled back from him reluctantly, swaying a little unsteadily on her feet. Her eyes widened on a point on his chest. 'There's blood on your shirt.'

He barely glanced down. 'It's fine.'

Much to her shame, his touch had stopped being comforting and had become something much more provocative long seconds ago—when the blood had rushed to intimate parts of her body in helpless reaction to being held by him. Her nipples were tight against the lace of her bra even now. Her skin was tingling all over and she felt hot.

He hadn't let her go completely. His hands were on her shoulders, his gaze searching hers. 'Where do you think you're going?'

Maddie met his eyes reluctantly, afraid he might see something of that shameful desire in her eyes. She felt very raw and exposed. 'I should go back to my hotel.' She shuddered reflexively, despite wanting to appear in control of her emotions. 'I want to have a shower. I feel dirty.'

When she moved to pull free of his hands completely Nic let her go, but to Maddie's horror her legs were so weak that they gave way. As if without his touch she couldn't stay standing.

Nic caught her up into his arms so fast her head spun, and he said grimly, 'You're not going anywhere. You're coming with me.'

Maddie tried to protest, but she was too weak. Being

in Nic's arms like this made her feel like the worst traitor for giving in, but she couldn't drum up the will to fight.

She was barely aware of Nic taking her into a lift and it ascending to the top floor, or their walk down the corridor and then a door swinging open onto a dimly lit room with a plush interior and stupendous views over night-time Buenos Aires.

Gently he put her down on a sofa and said, 'Will you be all right for a minute?'

Maddie nodded, feeling guilty. The minute Nic had enfolded her in his arms she'd felt a thousand times better. He stood up to his full height and Maddie watched as he picked up a phone. With his other hand he yanked off his bow tie and shucked off his jacket. He opened the top buttons of his shirt with long, lean fingers, and Maddie's mouth went dry.

He was speaking in low tones on the phone. 'Send up a first-aid kit, please? Thank you.'

He put down the phone and disappeared into the bathroom. Maddie could hear running water, and then Nic reappeared. He squatted down beside her. 'Do you feel okay to have a shower?'

Maddie's skin was still crawling when she thought of that man. She nodded vigorously and Nic helped her up from the couch.

He said, 'There's a robe in the bathroom. By the time you're out I'll have a first-aid kit to see to your lip.'

Maddie went into the steam-filled bathroom and shut the door. She leant back against it for a long moment, until the steam started to make her feel light-headed. Incredibly weary, she undressed and stepped into the shower, letting the hot water beat down for a long time before soaping up her hands and washing herself all over. Finally, when she felt clean again, she got out.

She dried herself and rubbed her hair, leaving it to hang damply down her back. Belting the robe tightly around her body, she cautiously opened the door again to face Nic.

He was standing with his back to her, looking out of one of the huge windows. Maddie's heart picked up its unsteady pace when he turned around to face her. He was drinking amber liquid from a tumbler glass but he put it down, coming towards her.

'Let me see your lip.'

Maddie put a finger to it and winced because it felt so swollen. Nic came and took her chin in his thumb and forefinger, lifting it to the light. Maddie held her breath. His proximity was setting every nerve tingling. She was intrigued and unsettled to see this side of him. He let her go and took some cotton wool and antiseptic from the first-aid kit.

'This might sting a bit.'

He touched the cotton wool to her lip and Maddie sucked in a breath, her eyes watering, but she said nothing.

'At least it's stopped bleeding. It'll have gone down by tomorrow.'

Maddie said, half jokingly, 'You're familiar with split lips, then?'

To her surprise Nic's jaw tightened. He just said, 'I've had a few in my time.'

Then something else caught Maddie's eye, and before she knew what she was doing she'd taken Nic's hand in hers. 'What's happened to your knuckles?' They were badly grazed.

When he tried to take his hand back Maddie held on firmly and looked at him.

Nic answered tightly, 'While you were in the shower I paid a visit to Morales.'

Maddie gasped. 'You hit him?'

Nic's face was hard, making a shiver run through Maddie.

'I stopped myself from knocking him senseless. He's lucky he got away with a bruised jaw.'

Overcome with a burgeoning and volatile emotion, Maddie bent her head and pressed a kiss to Nic's bruised knuckles. She looked up again and said huskily, 'I hate violence, but in this case...thank you.'

Nic's eyes were so blue Maddie felt as if she was falling, even though she was still standing. A taut stillness came into the air around them—until Nic said, 'Morales is claiming that you slept with him.'

For a second Maddie almost didn't understand what he was saying, and then the words sank in—and the way Nic was looking at her. She dropped his hand, suddenly aghast that she'd just kissed it. She'd been looking at him like some lovestruck groupie and he still thought...

Maddie felt sick.

'You think I'm lying.' Her voice was flat. She moved back, conscious of being in a hotel robe with nothing underneath. And of having exposed herself. How could she have forgotten for a moment, just because Nic had been slightly chivalrous and protective, that he still didn't trust her, that he thought the worst of her? He'd done nothing he wouldn't have done for any other distressed woman. She'd just read an ocean of meaning into his actions...

In the ensuing silence Maddie looked away. Even if she reiterated her innocence it would be her word against Morales's. She looked back at Nic again, and said half defiantly, 'What do you care anyway?'

Nic felt a heavy dark weight lodge in his gut. He *had* believed Maddie, out there in the corridor, when she'd been so obviously distraught. But when he'd confronted Morales just now and the man had drunkenly goaded Nic by saying, 'Jealous, de Rojas? Because she slept with me and not you?' Nic had seen red. He hadn't been so angry in years. Before he'd even known what he was doing his fist had connected with Morales's smirking face.

It burned Nic inside to know that he'd been driven to violence—not so much by what the man had done to Maddie as at the thought that she might have actually slept with him.

Just now, when she'd taken his bruised hand in hers and kissed his knuckles and then looked up at him, he'd felt as if he was drowning in those green depths. Losing himself in her. Again. The last time he'd lost himself with this woman she'd annihilated him.

He assured himself that he was not that young man any more. But it was as if she'd peeled back a protective layer of his skin, exposing his innermost self all over again.

Pushing down that heavy weight even further, Nic said coolly, 'I care about the fact that a man abused you. Beyond that it's none of my business.'

Maddie was incredibly hurt by Nic's mistrust, and couldn't believe that she'd been so seduced by a little tenderness. Once again Nic was proving just how naive she was—as if Alex Morales hadn't already drummed it into her.

'You're right.' She hoped she matched his cool tone. 'It is none of your business.'

Maddie went to go back into the bathroom to get her dress.

Nic said from behind her in a curt voice, 'Where are you going?'

She turned around. 'I have to return to my hotel. My bus back to Mendoza leaves at six tomorrow morning.'

Nic emitted a curse that made Maddie blush. And then

he said curtly, 'You're not going back to that hotel. It's too late. And you're coming home with me tomorrow. You will *not* be taking a sixteen-hour bus journey again.'

Maddie felt like stamping her foot. Why couldn't Nic just disapprove of her and let her go?

Volatile emotions were rising, making her voice wobbly. 'I might have believed you care if you hadn't just accused me of sleeping with a man to secure his favour. A man capable of violence! Quite frankly my cockroach-infested hotel room is a more enticing prospect than staying here to suffer your judgemental condemnation.'

Nic slashed a hand through the air. 'Dammit, Maddie, I'll get another room. But you're *not* leaving this hotel—and if I have to lock you in here, I will. Tell me where your stuff is.'

Maddie looked at Nic and fumed—inwardly and outwardly. She put her hands on her hips. 'Damn *you*, Nic de Rojas. You think you're so perfect? How dare you pretend to be honourable when you clearly think me nothing better than a street—'

Nic closed the distance between them in seconds. Suddenly he was too close and Maddie backed away, her pulse leaping in her throat. He was blisteringly angry—but Maddie sensed that it wasn't with *her.* That threw her.

'Your hotel and your room number, Maddie. I'm not going to take no for an answer.'

To her everlasting mortification, when Maddie thought of navigating Buenos Aires to get to her fleapit of a hotel, and that tortuous bus journey tomorrow, she wanted to cry. She was still feeling extremely fragile and vulnerable. Nic thought she had sold herself this evening for her estate, and yet he'd insisted on looking after her—as if she was an unsavoury package he had to take care of. She could see the glitter of determination in his eyes, and wouldn't put it past him to lock her into the suite.

She swallowed and gritted out finally, 'It's the Hotel Esmerelda. Room 410.'

Nic was returning to the suite after booking another room for himself and getting Maddie's things from her hotel. He'd wanted to get away from her so that his brain might start functioning again in a vaguely normal manner.

Deep down he didn't really believe that she'd slept with Morales…but when she stood in front of him and those green eyes were on his the need to put up a wall between them felt like the most important thing. He'd had no defence when he'd seen her so upset and vulnerable, and the speed and ease with which she got under his skin terrified him.

Nic steeled himself outside the suite door. He had her one small suitcase in his hands, pathetically light. Any woman he knew travelled with a veritable entourage to carry their luggage. But not Maddie.

When he opened the door and went in all was hushed. He'd half expected to see her standing defiantly where he'd left her. He explored further and came to a halt. She was curled up on the couch like a little lost soul, black hair fanned over her shoulders, her head resting on one arm.

Nic's chest constricted and he put down the bag. He walked over and bent down beside her, but she didn't stir. Overcome with a feeling too huge to push down, Nic tucked some black silky locks behind her ear. She was so pale, her eyebrows starkly black against her skin. That garish cut looked even more lurid.

Unable to help himself, Nic bent forward and pressed a kiss to the corner of her mouth where it was cut.

Maddie was asleep, but in her dreams something amazing was happening. She felt cocooned in safety and warmth and something else—something much hotter. Desire. She dreamt that Nic was touching his lips to hers gently, lingering as if he couldn't force himself to pull away.

Maddie struggled up through layers of consciousness and opened slumberous eyes. She was looking directly into Nic's vivid blue eyes, intent on hers with a seriousness that connected with something deep inside her. She wasn't even sure if she was dreaming or not.

She moved her mouth experimentally, loath to lose that connection of his warm firm mouth on hers. Gently he applied more pressure, and Maddie's lips opened slightly. Her eyes fluttered closed, because the sheer intensity of his gaze was too much. She felt the tip of his tongue exploring, and a deep mewl sounded in the back of her throat. Instinctively she sank back even further into the couch, aware of Nic's broad chest close to her breasts.

The pressure of his mouth on hers became stronger, and a fire started fizzing in her veins. Maddie angled her head and Nic's hands and fingers sank into her hair, cupping her head so that he could stroke his tongue inside her mouth and tease hers.

Maddie felt buoyant. Euphoria was infecting her blood. When Nic's mouth left hers and he trailed his lips down over her chin and neck her head fell back, her belly tightening with need. If she was dreaming she never wanted to wake up. She could feel his head descending and he pulled open her robe. Maddie felt air whistle over the exposed slope of her breast, and her hands were on Nic's shoulders, as if to hold him in place.

She raised her heavy head and looked down to see Nic's own dark blond one close to the pale swell. With his hand he was exposing her breast fully now, and cupping the plump mound with its tight pink nipple. A callused thumb circled the darker areola and then flicked the tip. Maddie sucked in a breath, her hands tightening on Nic's shoulders. Her body was arching towards him, instinctively seeking more.

When his mouth moved down to take the place of his thumb and surrounded her with a moist sucking heat she gasped out loud. Never had she felt such an intense building need within her...at least not since that cataclysmic week after which everything had changed and been tainted.

Her urgency seemed to be transmitting itself to Nic. His mouth became rougher and his hand moved down, sliding under her robe, over her belly and down. His mouth came back up to find hers, but they'd both lost sight of the fact that Maddie was injured—because pain bloomed as soon as Nic's mouth crushed to hers.

It was like a shower of cold water being thrown down on them both. Maddie yelped with pain and Nic sprang back as if shot. Maddie put her hand to her mouth and felt the warm trickle of blood again. She all but scrambled off the couch, feeling totally disorientated. *How* had she ended up kissing Nic?

Maddie wasn't even comforted by the sight of his own flushed cheeks and tortured expression. She went to the bathroom and straight to the mirror. There wasn't much blood. She sucked in a shaky breath and wet the corner of a facecloth to hold it to her mouth. Her eyes were huge and glittering, her cheeks hectic with colour. Her chest was rising and falling as if she'd just been running, and down lower, between her legs, she was slippery, hot and aching. His hand had been so close...those long fingers almost touching her right there. She pressed her legs together as if that would push down the desire.

When she felt a little more in control of herself she went

back outside to see Nic standing like a statue, watching her warily.

'I think I'd like to be alone now.'

Something savage crossed Nic's face, and in two long strides he was right in front of her. 'You wanted it too, Maddie. Don't pretend you didn't.'

Maddie flushed. Okay, so she'd woken up to find Nic's mouth on hers, but the kiss had been supremely gentle. She could remember the moment when she could have drawn back and pushed him away, but weakly she'd wanted to pretend that she didn't have to make the decision to stop and had exerted pressure back, changing it into a very mutual thing.

The hurt of his low opinion of her was still raw. Maddie had to protect herself. For him this was just sexual attraction. He didn't even care that she might have slept with another man only hours before.

Nic reached his hand out as if to touch her lip and Maddie jerked back, making his eyes flash dangerously.

'It's fine. Please, Nic, just go.'

He looked at her for a long moment, a muscle pulsing in his jaw, and then finally he stepped back. 'Eight in the morning I'll come and get you. Be ready.'

Maddie nodded.

Nic turned and walked towards the main door, and then he turned back. Ominously he said, 'We're not done with this, Maddie. Not by a long shot.'

CHAPTER SEVEN

MADDIE was grateful that Nic seemed preoccupied the next morning, and their journey to the airfield was made largely in silence. He'd looked at her assessingly this morning, and Maddie had had to submit to his inspection of her mouth, her chin in his hand as he'd tipped her face up to him.

Just the touch of those fingers to her face had had her heating up inside like an exploding thermostat. He'd let her go and declared, 'The swelling has gone down. A couple more days and you won't even see it.'

Maddie had bitten back the childish urge to tell him that she could have figured that out for herself, but a weak part of her had *liked* his concern. Even if it was only perfunctory.

The small private jet was all cream leather seats and pristinely carpeted luxury. Maddie was intimidated by this further evidence of Nic's wealth. He, however, was nonchalant, his large frame dominating a two-seater couch along one wall. Maddie chose a seat at right angles to Nic.

When they were airborne, and Maddie had turned down the offer of champagne, the silence grew taut between them. Maddie wished she had a book or something to pretend an interest in. She was far too aware of Nic brooding just feet away, and felt like asking snappishly what was wrong.

She risked a glance over and her heart flipped in her chest. Instead of a censorious blue gaze she saw his head tipped back and his eyes closed. His jaw was tense, though, so he couldn't be asleep. She could see the dark fans his lashes made on those defined cheekbones, the faint stubble already forming on his jaw even though he was freshly shaved.

His shirt was open at the neck and Maddie had a tantalising glimpse of dark blond chest hair dusting dark olive skin. She looked back up and blanched when she saw him staring back at her. She'd just been caught ogling him like some lust-crazed teenage girl.

Despite his relaxed pose, Maddie could sense that inwardly he was alert, like an animal poised to strike. Immediately she felt nervous.

'I have a proposition for you.'

Maddie felt even more nervous. She cleared her throat and crossed her legs. 'What kind of a proposition?'

His eyes flicked down briefly to follow the movement of her legs, and Maddie pressed her thighs together unconsciously. Nic took his arms off the back of the couch and moved forward, resting his arms on his thighs.

'I think you've proved how determined you are to save your estate.'

Maddie flushed to think of the awful helplessness she'd felt in Alex Morales's room, how easily he'd dominated her. How easily he could have hurt her far worse than he had.

Defensively she said, 'I wouldn't do what I did last night again. It was stupid.'

Nic shrugged minutely. 'You were just out of your depth.'

Maddie stung at Nic's rebuke, but it was true. She wanted to get them off the subject of last night. It reminded her of too much raw emotion. 'What is it you want to pro-pose?'

For a split second Maddie had an image in her head of Nic kneeling at her feet, looking at her with a tortured expression and asking her to marry him. Hot colour seeped into her cheeks, making his gaze narrow on hers, and Maddie wished she could just disappear.

'You still insist on seeking an investor—you won't sell?'

Maddie tensed. She shook her head. 'I'll never sell.'

'So,' he prodded, 'you'll keep looking for an investor?'

Maddie nodded. 'I have to.'

Grimly Nic said, 'That's what I was afraid of.'

Wary now, Maddie said, 'What do you mean?'

Nic was shaking his head. 'You're not going to find it easy. Morales is undoubtedly making sure your name is muck. If he told *me* last night that you'd slept together, then he'll be spreading the word to others too.'

Maddie felt sick. She wanted to shout and scream her innocence to Nic, but she knew he wouldn't listen to her.

'So...what does that mean?'

Nic said, 'It means that unless you go to Europe and seek out your contacts there you don't have a hope of getting an investor.'

Maddie felt sicker. She had no money for a trip like that, and she couldn't go and ask her old boss for help. He had a flourishing business, but not enough to invest the kind of money she needed. And she'd left him after he'd put her through college. She could hardly ask him for a handout when he'd already been so generous.

Maddie looked at Nic. She felt incredibly bleak. 'So what is this? An exercise in showing me how hopeless my case is?'

Nic looked at Maddie. He had her exactly where he wanted her now. Well, not *exactly*. Where he really wanted her was on her back, underneath him, begging for release. But this was a means to that end. He felt ruthless, but he quashed the feeling. Last night had proved to him how out of control he was around Maddie as soon as he came within touching distance.

He had to have her. But he had to protect himself in the process. He needed to control this vulnerability. And what he was about to propose offered him that protection.

Nic watched her reaction closely as he said, 'I will invest in your estate.'

The colour seemed to leach from Maddie's cheeks at first, leaving her skin like porcelain and her eyes huge. And then, as she took a deep breath, colour rushed back, staining those cheeks red. His groin throbbed in response.

She shook her head. 'No way. You want something. You want to ruin me.'

Nic smiled. 'I have to admit that at first I just wanted you gone...but since you've come home life has certainly been more entertaining.'

Maddie resolutely turned away and crossed her arms over her chest. Nic's eyes were helplessly drawn to where her breasts were pushed up, clearly defined under the thin T-shirt she wore. One long lock of black hair curled down, tantalisingly close to the slope of her breast, and he clenched his jaw. He had to have this woman. He would go insane if he didn't.

Maddie seethed inwardly. So Nic thought she was *entertaining*? She heard a movement and in seconds he'd come to sit in the empty chair opposite hers. His long legs were stretched out on either side of hers, effectively caging her in.

'What do you think you're doing?' Maddie gritted out.

Nic smiled easily. 'I'm going to make you see that you have no option but to give in to my proposal. Unless you want to see your estate fall apart and your staff left with nothing after their long years of hard work.'

Maddie's mouth had opened, but now she shut it again. Hernan and Maria. They had nothing but the security she provided them with. Not even pay.

As if reading her mind, Nic said softly, 'If you let me invest in the Vasquez estate, Hernan and Maria will be secure. I will set up a pension plan. Hernan can work on the vines again. You can hire a new head winemaker.' Before she could say anything he went on, 'You need new barrels, and we both know how much they cost. The last I heard your father was still using a basket press.'

Maddie flushed hotly. Her father had favoured the old-school methods. Defensively she said, 'The basket press is coming back into vogue.'

Nic inclined his head. 'I'm not denying that. I use one myself for certain grapes. But you can't use a basket press alone. It has to be a sideline to a much more modern operation. It's a luxury—like hand-picking your crop.'

'*You* still hand-pick,' Maddie shot back.

'Yes, I do, but again that's only for certain grapes. Most of our picking is done by machines now.'

Maddie felt an ache near her heart. What Nic had on his estate was a blending of the old and the modern, which was exactly the way she would love to see things run on the Vasquez estate.

He went on relentlessly. 'Not all your vines are ruined. You have a hope of a respectable harvest next year if you take care of your vines now and cut them back. And what about the vines that have produced something? How are you going to harvest them with only yourself and Hernan?'

Maddie felt a sinking weight in her belly. She couldn't take her gaze off Nic's. It was glued there in some kind of sick fascination. He was chipping away at all the walls surrounding her, showing her the huge gaping holes where they all threatened to fall down on top of her.

'I'll draw up a contract, so it'll be a legal document. I will invest in your estate, see to the provision of labour and materials, new machinery. I will oversee the production of your first fully functioning harvest, whether that's next year or the year after, and then I will stand back and let you take over.'

Maddie looked at him suspiciously. 'You'll walk away?'

Nic smiled cynically. 'Not without a large share of the profits each year, Maddie, until the investment is paid off. You won't see much of an income for a while, but it'll give you your estate back and protect your staff.'

Somewhere deep inside Maddie a tiny seed of hope and excitement was blooming. What Nic was offering was more than generous.

The tiny seed disappeared at the thought of Nic overseeing everything, being autocratic.

'You'd turn the Vasquez estate into a subsidiary of your own.'

Remarkably, he shook his head. 'That's not what I'm interested in. I quite like the idea of helping foster some healthy competition again, and I'm interested to see how you would develop things.'

Somehow Maddie couldn't see Nic deferring to her judgement. Suspiciously she asked, 'Would you state that in the contract?'

He nodded once. 'Of course. It'll all be laid out in black and white. You can read over it with your own legal people.'

Maddie held back a moment of hysteria. She had no money for legal people. She and Hernan would just have to vet it as best they could. That thought gave her a jolt. Was she already taking this as a given? She hated it that

Nic could manipulate her so easily, but at the same time she wasn't stupid enough to cut her nose off to spite her face.

Stiffly she said, 'I'd have to think about it.'

Nic smiled tersely. 'There's not much to think about, Maddie. I'm offering you a chance to sink or swim.'

After that comment, Nic settled back in his seat and stretched out his legs, trapping Maddie even more. He put back his head and within minutes was snoring softly. Finally Maddie could relax slightly. She uncrossed her arms. Her head was buzzing with all that Nic had just said and offered.

She looked suspiciously at his benignly sleeping face. He had to have an agenda. It couldn't be this simple.

She looked out of the window at the vast pampas lands underneath them. This was what she'd always wanted more than anything—a chance to work on her own estate. It had been denied her her whole life, and when her father had finally offered her the chance it had come too late. And now Nic de Rojas, the most unlikely person on the planet, was offering her a second chance. Not only that, but she had a responsibility to her staff. Hernan and Maria couldn't live on the estate indefinitely. Soon they would want to retire. They were old and weary.

Maddie sighed again, and then finally let her own weariness suck her under into sleep.

'Maddie...'

Maddie woke with a start. She'd been dreaming about Nic. Her cheek was tingling, as if someone had just touched her there. When her eyes focused, Nic was bending down so close to her that she could see the small lines fanning out from his eyes. She felt too hot, and knew instantly that it had been an erotic dream.

Scrabbling back into her seat as far as she could, she saw his jaw clench.

'We're landing in a few minutes. Buckle up.'

Maddie buckled up with trembling hands, relieved that Nic had moved back over to the couch. She could breathe a little easier when he wasn't in her direct line of sight.

They landed softly and within minutes were in Nic's Jeep, heading out of Mendoza and towards Villarosa. Maddie felt as if she'd done ten rounds in a boxing ring—mentally and physically. She snuck a look at Nic's rigid profile. He looked so stern. Had she just imagined what had happened on the plane? Had he really told her he'd invest?

When the familiar lines of the Vasquez estate came into view Maddie breathed a sigh of relief. Nic stopped at the steps leading up to the main door. He indicated the house. 'Renovation of the house would be part of the investment too.'

Maddie's heart thumped. She hadn't imagined it. She looked at him warily. 'Why are you doing this?'

Nic's face was suspiciously expressionless. He shrugged minutely. 'I have the means…and I don't like to see a good vineyard turn to dust.'

Maddie struggled to understand. She couldn't do this unless she knew *why.* She turned in her seat to face Nic. 'But our families…the feud…we've fought for so long. How do I know you're not going to just take me over completely?'

Nic's mouth tightened, and something ambiguous flashed in his eyes. 'You once told me that the feud meant nothing to you.'

Maddie felt very vulnerable thinking of that time. 'You said the same thing. But then…it all blew up again.'

Nic looked impossibly stern. 'Our parents are dead, Maddie. It's just us now. I'm willing to move on if you are.'

Maddie didn't trust him for a second. She saw something else light his eyes and immediately her insides tightened.

'There is one condition to my offer—and it won't be in the contract.'

Instantly Maddie's hackles rose. She breathed out. 'I knew it was too good to be true. So what is this condition?'

After a long moment, during which Maddie's nerves were screaming with tension, Nic finally said softly, 'One night with me, Maddie. One night in my bed to finish what was started eight years ago.'

Maddie looked at Nic disbelievingly. She knew what was between them. It crackled in the air the moment they came within feet of each other, and she'd been moments away from begging him to take her only last night... But somehow she'd been hoping that she could ignore it.

Now Nic had laid it between them. He had made the business proposition about this heat between them. She shook her head. Her throat felt tight. 'Whether you believe me or not, a man offered me a similar deal last night and I turned him down. What makes you think this is any different?'

Nic leant forward, and Maddie couldn't move back any further. The door handle was pressing painfully into her back. Nic was so close now she could feel his breath on her face. He trailed a finger down her cheek and lower, pushing aside the top of her T-shirt to rest it where the pulse was nearly beating out of her skin. His forearm touched her breast, making the nipple spring into aching hardness, pushing against the fabric of her bra.

Nic smiled, and as if he knew exactly what was happening to her body, he subtly moved his forearm back and forth against that turgid peak.

'This is different, Maddie, because you didn't want him.

You want me...so badly I can smell it. And *that's* why you'll do this.'

Panic rose up inside Maddie, almost strangling her. She reached behind her and fumbled for the door handle, almost landing on her backside outside the Jeep in her haste. Nic was out too, and coming towards her. It took a minute for Maddie to realise he was holding out her bag. She grabbed it from him inelegantly.

Nic smiled and just said, 'You know where I am, Maddie. I look forward to hearing from you. That is,' he added softly, 'if you're interested in saving your estate and being honest with yourself.'

And then he got back into his Jeep and drove off, leaving a small cloud of dust in his wake.

For almost a week Maddie battled sleepless nights full of demons and Nic's voice saying, *Be honest with yourself.* She spent the long days facing the fact that without funds she and Hernan could make nothing even of the small harvest they could bring in.

She went round and round in her head, endlessly replaying her last conversation with Nic word for word, and always with a flash of heat she came back to him saying, *'You want me...so badly I can smell it. And that's why you'll do this.'*

She did want him. She couldn't deny that. She wasn't that much of a hypocrite. It scared her the way the days dragged, and how her mind kept returning to him like iron filings to a magnet. She hadn't realised how accustomed she'd become to seeing him, or expecting him to turn up. And when he didn't...she didn't like the feeling of emptiness.

Maddie desperately tried not to think about his *condition* to the investment proposal, but invariably she would

think about it. In a way, the thought of doing it like this...
where the lines were clearly marked in the sand, with no
false emotions involved, no false seduction...should actually make it easier.

Maddie knew that when it came to Nic de Rojas she was
weak. He could have put on an elaborate act, pretended to
seduce her. And she would have fallen for it. She knew she
would have. And in the process she would have shown him
how ambiguous her feelings were for him. This way there
was no ambiguity. She was protected. She would gain closure finally, and shut the door on that part of her life. The
awful memories surrounding what had happened might
finally fade into the background and she could move on.

Maddie weakly blocked out the fact that she'd have to
deal with him every day for a long time to come if she
agreed to this. It would make the prospect of closure all but
redundant. But as the days passed Maddie was no closer
to being able to pick up the phone and change the course
of her life irrevocably.

At the end of the week, late in the evening, Maddie
was sitting in her father's study, brooding that she was
only able to see the documents in front of her because Nic
was paying for the electricity, when Hernan came in. He
looked concerned.

'I'm worried about you...and this place.' He was shaking his head. 'We're backed up against the wall, Maddie.
There's nothing you can do. You'll have to sell up.'

For a moment Maddie clung to that like a life raft. 'But
what about you and Maria?'

She could see how Hernan paled slightly in the dim
light. He shrugged, but Maddie wasn't fooled by his non-
chalance. 'Don't worry about us, *niña*. We can take care
of ourselves. You're not responsible for us.'

Maddie felt hope die and a heavy weight almost crushed

her. She knew how much this estate owed Hernan. He was such a gifted viticulturist that he alone had been responsible for the quality of their grapes, which had allowed her father and his chief winemaker to come up with the successful blends that had led to their wealth and security. She couldn't turn her back on Hernan now, or his wife. And she knew she couldn't turn her back on the very legacy she held in her hands.

'We might not have to sell...'

Immediately Hernan sat up straight. 'What do you mean?'

Maddie laid out the bare facts of Nic's investment plan without mentioning his private little caveat which affected only her.

Hernan looked at her incredulously. 'But...you will say yes, won't you? It's a chance to save the Vasquez name—the *only* chance.'

Maddie looked at Hernan. 'It's such a huge step to take. How do I know I can trust him?'

Maddie knew she wasn't talking about the investment itself now. She was talking about whether or not she could trust Nic not to sleep with her and decimate her completely. She was talking about whether or not she could trust herself not to lose herself completely if she took that cataclysmic step.

Hernan sagged in his seat and suddenly looked ten years older. Maddie immediately forgot about everything. 'Hernan, what is it?'

He looked up eventually, and his face was ashen. 'The truth is, Maddie, Maria isn't well. She needs treatment—treatment that we can't afford.'

Maddie got up and went over and put her arms around Hernan. He said to her with tears in his eyes, 'We didn't want you to worry... We thought the only option would be to sell and we would leave and go to our son in Buenos Aires.'

Maddie immediately shook her head. She knew that Hernan and Maria hated the city. Their lives were here. Their son in Buenos Aires was not well off, and had a family of his own to look after.

'There's absolutely no way you're going anywhere. If I agree to this deal with Nic de Rojas, I'll make sure you're both looked after—and especially Maria.'

Hernan took her hand in his old and worn ones. 'But we don't want to put you under pressure...we're not your responsibility.'

Maddie squatted down so that she could look at Hernan properly. She squeezed his hand and said, 'I know that, Hernan, but you are due something for all your years of service. You deserve medical care, at the very least, and security. I can provide that now.' She took a deep breath. 'I'll call Nic de Rojas tonight.'

Hernan gripped her hand tightly, the sheen of tears still in his eyes, and Maddie felt emotional. She'd done it now. No going back. She couldn't even if she wanted to. These people were more important to her than her own petty personal concerns.

The following evening Maddie was driving over to Nic's estate, an overnight bag in the back. She was so tense she felt as if she might crack apart, and she forced herself to breathe deep. It had been a tumultuous and emotional day.

The previous evening she'd rung Nic and told him she'd agree to the investment with the proviso that he met a condition of her own—that Maria be taken care of with the best medical care as soon as possible. Nic hadn't hesitated. He'd agreed immediately, and it had struck another blow to Maddie's misconceptions about him.

That morning Nic had appeared with his own doctor, who had consulted with Hernan and Maria. Maria had been taken into the best private clinic in Mendoza that very afternoon, and the relief they'd both felt had been palpable to Maddie. She'd been incredibly emotional as she'd watched them leave.

Maddie was aghast at how relieved she'd felt to see Nic arriving that morning, along with intense fizzing excitement in every cell. It had felt as if she hadn't seen him in months, not days. When she'd seen him up close, though, he'd looked a little worn and tired. Maddie had had to quash the ridiculous urge to ask him if everything was all right.

When Hernan and Maria had left Maddie had faced Nic, feeling extremely vulnerable. 'Thank you for taking care of Maria...it was important to Hernan and to me.'

'Don't mention it.'

Reluctantly she'd asked him, there on the steps of the house. 'So what happens now...?'

He'd just looked at her with an expression so intense that Maddie had gone slowly redder and redder.

'You will come to me this evening. Eight p.m.'

He'd said nothing else. He'd walked to his Jeep, got in and left.

Maddie forced herself to concentrate on the road now and tried not think about what the night would bring.

Nic was pacing in his office. He did not like to admit how close to panic he'd been by yesterday evening when Maddie had finally rung. The very walls of his house had been closing in on him, and he hadn't liked his clawing desperation to see her again. He'd hated not knowing what she was up to—had she gone looking for another investor? Had she somehow miraculously secured an investor without his knowing?

Nic had agreed as soon as she'd mentioned wanting Maria to be taken care of. He would have agreed to anything except Maddie reneging on their own personal part of the agreement. That she would be his for one night.

One night. Nic stopped pacing and looked out over his vineyard which was disappearing into the dusk, the colours melding and blurring. One night. He could do this. One night was invariably all it took for him to grow bored with a woman. So why would Maddie be different? His conscience pricked. Who was he kidding? Maddie had been different from the moment his hormones had realised she was growing up.

Nic ran a hand through his hair impatiently and turned around. A sheaf of papers sat on his desk. It was the investment contract. It epitomised everything Nic couldn't articulate about this woman who had come back into his life. This woman who he wanted more than the breath he took into his body. He hadn't realised how starved he'd been for her until he'd heard her voice on the phone the previous evening. Even though she'd been cool, he'd been burning up just to hear her.

And then when he'd seen her today…he'd wanted to back her into the wall of the house and take her there and then. His desire was like a wild beast, clawing at his insides.

This contract meant that Maddie would not turn around after tonight and claim that she'd been *bored*, or that she regretted what happened. Because she couldn't. She wanted her estate too badly. And she wanted Nic too badly too— even though he knew without the contract she might deny it. This way she couldn't. He would not be exposed again. Never again.

So why, when Nic looked at the sheaf of papers on his desk, did they seem to mock him?

Maddie looked warily at the big pink box with the red satin bow which sat on the bed as if it might jump up and bite her. She'd arrived at Nic's house and been met by Geraldo, who had greeted her warmly and shown her up to a sumptuous suite of rooms—as if they didn't both know she was there to spend the night with Nic.

He'd indicated to the lavish box on the bed and said, 'A gift from Señor de Rojas. He'll see you in the dining room at eight. If you need anything in the meantime please don't hesitate to call.'

Eventually, aware of time passing, Maddie opened it up and peeled back layers of blood-red tissue paper to reveal what seemed to be acres of dark grey satin folds. She lifted the dress out and gasped. It was stunning. No woman could be immune to the beauty of a dress like this. The material was heavy, and yet as light as a feather. Strapless, it had a ruched bodice and a high waist, and it fell in swathes of satin and chiffon layers to the ground.

More was hidden in the tissue paper in the box: silver shoes with diamanté straps and dark grey underwear, lacy and ethereal. There was also a velvet box, and Maddie opened it to reveal stunning teardrop diamond earrings and a matching bracelet. Something very fragile inside her withered slightly when she looked at the incredible bounty of luxurious goods laid out on the bed. But then Maddie chastised herself. Nic was actually doing her a favour, treating her like a mistress. All she had to do tonight was play a part—perhaps that would help her to stay intact and immune to emotion.

At eight o'clock on the dot Maddie was standing nervously at the door of the room a shy young girl had indicated. The dress felt unbelievably decadent against Maddie's bare legs. She'd put on the underwear simply because she had nothing else to wear that wouldn't ruin the line of the dress. The jewellery felt heavy and cold against her skin.

She'd put on the minimum of makeup and left her hair down—primarily because her hands were shaking too much to do anything more elaborate. Taking a deep breath and trying to remain in a detached frame of mind, Maddie knocked lightly on the door before opening it.

The scene inside was impossibly seductive, with candles flickering and a small table set for two. It was a different room from the one they'd eaten in before, more formal. It took a second for Maddie to register Nic standing by the window, his hands in his pockets. He was dressed semi-formally in a white shirt and dark trousers, hair slicked back and damp, as if he'd just had a shower.

'You wore the dress.'

Maddie gripped the handle hard and struggled to maintain her equilibrium in the face of this seductive scene. She bit back the need to remind him that she was just playing the part he wanted. 'Yes, thank you.'

Nic inclined his head and smiled faintly. 'You can let go of the door. I won't bite. I promise.'

Heat bloomed inside Maddie at the thought of Nic's teeth nipping her sensitive flesh. She let the door go abruptly just as a staff member came into the room. After conferring with Nic for a moment the man left again, and Nic walked over to the antique sideboard which held different bottles of drink.

She watched as he poured some champagne into two flutes. He came and offered her one and she took it.

He tipped his glass to hers, eyes unnervingly intense. *'Salud.'*

'*Salud,*' Maddie echoed, and took a sip of the sparkling effercescent drink, tearing her gaze away from Nic's to look around the room.

'Your mouth has healed well.'

Maddie looked back to Nic and instinctively touched the corner where it had split. It *had* healed.

'You look beautiful tonight.'

Something uncomfortable was prickling across Maddie's skin. She wasn't used to this—to compliments. To Nic being so effortlessly urbane around her. She didn't know how to behave. And all she could think of was how beautiful *he* looked.

'So do you,' she answered huskily, and then blushed and looked down. 'That is, not beautiful but handsome.'

Oh, God. Maddie took another quick sip of her drink before she could make a complete blithering idiot of herself. She wasn't sophisticated. Surely Nic could see that?

To fill the yawning gap in conversation Maddie asked if Nic had had any news from the hospital about Maria, and he told her that they were still doing tests. Maria had gone to the local doctor with chest pains and they were concerned that it could be a heart problem.

'Thank you again,' Maddie said huskily. 'Hernan didn't know where to turn, and they couldn't have afforded the kind of care they're getting now.'

Sounding serious, Nic said, 'I pay for health insurance for all my employees. Maria and Hernan will be included in that too.'

Maddie had the suspicion that Nic would have helped them anyway. It made her uncomfortable to acknowledge this, so she said, slightly acerbically, 'Just like I'm going to be an employee?'

He chided her. 'Business partners, Maddie...'

Nic drained his glass of champagne and put it down,

gesturing for Maddie to be seated at the dinner table. It was ornately set, with gleaming silverware and crockery so delicate-looking that Maddie was afraid to touch it. The champagne was fizzing in her blood, making her feel slightly light-headed.

The whole scene was intimidating to Maddie.

Especially when Nic looked so sophisticated and at ease across the table from her.

Discreet staff came in and served them with their starter—a light soup. A sense of panic and claustrophobia was rising inside Maddie, and the soup became like treacle in her throat. It was as if they were both ignoring the elephant in the room. The fact that Nic expected them to have dinner and then go upstairs and have sex. At that moment Maddie couldn't even imagine Nic's expression changing from the stern one he'd had since she'd arrived.

Maddie was aware that her own wish to remain detached was fast dissolving.

More staff arrived to take their starters away. Maddie felt agitated and hot.

Nic frowned at her. 'Are you okay? You look a little flushed.'

It was the dispassionate way he asked that galvanised Maddie. She wanted to scream, *No, I'm not okay!* She stood up abruptly, making some of the crockery knock the wine glasses. It sounded like gunshots. She put out a trembling hand, only realising then how agitated she was. The sparkle of diamonds at her wrist was like cold fire.

'I…I can't do this like this. Pretending that this is normal when it's not.'

CHAPTER EIGHT

Nic was just looking at her. Maddie's skin was prickling all over. She started to take off the jewellery, all but ripping the undoubtedly expensive earrings from her ears and the bracelet off her wrist. Immediately she started to feel lighter.

'All this. It's not *me*. I can't sit here and act like nothing is happening...'

Nic stood too. Someone came into the room with a tray and Nic sent them a glowering look, making them disappear again. He looked back to Maddie, the expression in his eyes feral. 'Something's happening, all right. You will *not* do this, Maddie. It's too late to back out. If we don't have tonight, you have *nothing.*'

Maddie backed away from the table and stumbled slightly. She bent down and took off the shoes with heels like weapons. Her heart was hammering and she craved air, and space, and something more tangible than what was in this room right now.

'If we do this we do it my way. I can't do it like this...' She flung out a hand. 'This seduction scene, it's all fake... we both know that's not what this is about.'

Maddie turned and all but stumbled out through the door, picking up the dress, half running and half walking to the main front door. She heard a curse behind her and

Nic following. She didn't even know where she was going, but she got out through the front door and looked to her left, saw the stables in the distance. Suddenly she knew.

Maddie was in the stables and leading a horse out of a stall, putting a bridle on, when she heard an ominously low, 'What the hell do you think you're doing?'

She took a deep breath, turned to look at Nic and nearly quailed. But she straightened her shoulders. 'I'm not leaving. But if this is happening, it's happening my way.'

Maddie found a box and stepped up to swing herself up on the saddleless horse. Now she was looking down at Nic and her heart tripped. His hair shone dark gold under the lights. A horse whinnied nearby.

He seemed to battle something inwardly, and then he cursed again and she saw him throw off his dinner jacket and lead his own horse out of the stall. It was a massive black stallion. She saw the play of his impressive muscles underneath the thin material of his shirt and something euphoric bubbled up inside Maddie. She kicked her heels and her horse moved out of the stables. Outside, the sun had set a short time before and the sky was a beautiful bruised lilac colour, still quite light.

Rows and rows of vines stretched as far as the eye could see, and in the distance were the huge vats and outbuildings which housed the hub of Nic's empire. Maddie turned in the other direction and kicked the horse into a trot— away from the house, towards the border between their estates.

When she had enough space she picked it up to a canter, and soon she heard powerful hooves behind her. Maddie had always felt free on a horse. She didn't look back, half afraid to see Nic bearing down on her. The cooling evening air caressed her hot bare skin. The satin folds of the dress fell and moved around her legs with the motion of the horse.

She felt the huge black presence of Nic's stallion come alongside her, and then Nic was reaching forward to effortlessly take Maddie's reins and bring her and her horse to a juddering halt. She had to press her thighs tight to its back to stop from falling off.

She spluttered, 'What do you think—?'

'Where the hell are we going?' he asked, anger vibrating from him in waves.

Maddie's mouth opened and closed, her breath coming rapidly. She refused to let herself be intimidated. 'You *know* where we're going.'

For a split second she thought she saw something bleak cross Nic's face, and then it was gone and his eyes spat blue sparks. 'I'm not going there with you.'

Maddie yanked her reins out of Nic's hands. 'If you want me—if you want this night—then we *are* going there.'

Nic looked at Maddie. His breath was searing through his lungs and it wasn't because of exertion. He was burning up. She looked magnificent. He'd been in a daze since he'd seen her arrive in the dining room, more beautiful than any woman he'd ever seen before. When he'd thought she was walking out on him he'd been so panicked it had made him feel weak.

He wasn't in a daze now, though, when he thought of what she was suggesting, and he snarled, 'What *is* this? Some pathetic attempt to be poetic? Well, it's lost on me. I'd sooner have you in my bed. Or back there in the stables would do fine.'

Maddie clamped down on the pain she felt when he spoke so crudely. She shook her head and her horse pranced away a little, sensing her agitation. 'No, it's there...or nowhere.'

Suddenly she'd whirled the horse around and was cantering off at speed again. Nic cursed volubly. There was enough light in the gathering dusk but she could still miss a rock or stone and be thrown in an instant. Giving in, he spurred his own horse on to follow.

When he reached the orchard, *déjà vu* nearly made him dizzy. He'd consciously and unconsciously avoided this place like the plague for years. Maddie's horse was riderless, tied to a small tree, and she was standing there—just waiting. Exactly as she had been all those years ago. Except now she was a mature woman. Her shoulders were bare and white in the dusk, her hair like black satin. Her breasts were full against the silk of her dress.

He swung off his horse, feeling tight inside, and secured him to another tree. He walked towards her. Her eyes were huge. Her face was pale. He felt acutely exposed, but he was reluctant to let her see how much being back here affected him.

Now that she was standing here Maddie couldn't believe she'd made this mad dramatic gesture. She'd acted from a visceral need to break out of that oh, so polite dinner as if nothing was wrong.

Her voice was husky, her senses already reeling at Nic's scent and proximity. 'This is where it started and where it ends. Tonight. For ever.'

Nic looked huge in the gloom. As if he'd grown several inches and his muscles had become even bigger. Once again she had a bittersweet rush of emotion at the knowledge that he'd once been much more vulnerable. But then he came towards her and Maddie's breath caught in her throat.

He stopped a couple of feet away and watched her, and then drawled laconically, 'Well, what are you waiting for?'

His insouciance after the intense anger she'd just wit-

nessed made her want to lash out. For a moment she had
believed that coming back here might have affected him
emotionally.

She was completely unprepared for this, despite her
show of bravado. He thought she'd slept with Morales the
other night, so he had the erroneous idea that she was some
grand seductress, when she'd never done anything like this
in her life. And the reason she'd never done it was standing right in front of her. The scar of that last traumatic
day after such a heady, perfect week was etched into her
psyche. It had inhibited her from seeking out male com-
pany, too scared of rejection and irrationally scared of
horrific revelation.

Sudden anger flared that Nic hadn't had to go through
any of that…he'd blithely got on with his life. That anger
galvanised Maddie to march up to him. She grabbed his
shirt in her hands and pulled him down towards her.

Maddie searched blindly and inexpertly for his mouth,
eyes shut tight against the reality of what she was doing,
telling herself that she could divorce all emotion from
this event.

For a long moment Nic seemed just to suffer under
Maddie's gauche ministrations, and she nearly sobbed with
frustration against his closed lips. Surely he must be realising how inexperienced she was? He couldn't be turned
on by this?

But then he took control, and everything changed in an
instant. Hard arms of steel wrapped around her, binding
her to him like a vice. His mouth opened and grew hard,
plundering hers with an expertise that awed her, his tongue
tangling hotly with hers, forcing her head back onto his
arms. Exposing her throat to him.

Everything within her was becoming languid and hot,
while an urgent need clamoured for attention between her

legs. Her breasts were swelling against the silk of her dress and her arms were crushed against Nic's chest.

When he finally pulled away she felt drunk. She couldn't open her eyes for a long moment. His hands came up and framed her face. She finally opened her eyes to see two blue oceans right in front of her. Two hot and stormy oceans.

His thumbs traced her cheekbones and then he dipped his head again to hers, his mouth touching more softly this time, teeth nipping gently at her lips, making them sting before soothing them. There was something so unexpectedly tender about this that Maddie could feel the bottom dropping out of the pit of her stomach.

It reminded her of when he'd been so gentle and seductive before...before it had all turned sour. She felt tears prick the backs of her eyes and desperately fought not to let them fall. Nic's mouth caressed and kissed her throat and shoulders, moving down. His hands dropped to her back, moulding her waist and hips, coming down to cup her buttocks through the silk of her dress, lifting her slightly so that his erection was cradled between her legs.

She gasped and tried to pull back, the intimate move suddenly shocking. But he wouldn't release her, those blue eyes blazing down into hers as he subtly moved his body back and forth against her until she was breathing rapidly and moving restlessly against him.

Hunger was rising in her, erasing thoughts of the past, gnawing and desperate. She nearly sobbed with relief when she felt him lower her down to the soft grass underneath the trees, following her. Now Nic loomed over her like a golden-haired god. Eyes devouring her, slipping down, taking in her chest rising and falling rapidly.

He lifted a hand and smoothed the back of it over the top of her bodice. Maddie sucked in a breath when his knuckles brushed the swell of her breast. He reached around underneath her back and found the zip. Maddie lifted slightly to help, sucking in a breath when she felt him pull it down as much as he could.

Slowly he peeled the dress down to expose one breast, and Maddie bit her lip, fighting the urge to cover herself. She could see Nic's cheeks become flushed, his pupils dilating, and a heady feminine energy rushed through her. He *wanted* her. Unconsciously she moved, so that her breast pushed forward, and the ghost of a small smile played around his mouth. Reverently he cupped and moulded the pale flesh, making Maddie close her eyes. A rough thumb rubbed back and forth over one tight, puckered peak.

She didn't even realise she'd said anything until she heard his throaty, 'What do you want?'

She opened her eyes. The lids felt heavy. 'I want...' *You,* she wanted to say, but she stopped. It felt so raw.

'Do you want me to taste you?'

He didn't wait for an answer. He looked feverish now, his eyes glittering fiercely, his big hand and long fingers still caressing her breast and making her want to shout out with frustration and pleasure all at once.

He came over her more fully, pressing her down into the ground, his erection feeling even bigger and harder now. He dipped his head and his mouth unerringly closed around that taut peak, and then Maddie did cry. It was surrounded with fierce sucking heat. He was relentless, tugging it into his mouth, tongue swirling around it until it was so stiff and tight and sensitised that she cried out again, her hips moving restlessly against his.

Almost roughly Nic pulled down the bodice, fully exposing both breasts now, and paid homage to the other thrusting peak, driving Maddie mad with pleasure. Her head was thrashing back and forth, and she could feel one of Nic's hands move down and start to pull up her dress, bunching it around her thighs. She couldn't speak or think. She could only feel.

He shifted slightly and his fingers touched her where her panties felt damp between her legs. His head came up, and cool air whistled over the wet peak of her breast. Maddie was overheating.

She looked up to see Nic staring at her. His fingers started to move back and forth, pressing her panties against where she was so wet. She moaned. She felt so exposed and yet she craved it.

'You're ready for me, aren't you?'

Maddie nodded, feeling vulnerable all of a sudden. She felt as if she'd been ready for him for years. Aeons.

'Tell me how much you want me right now.'

Maddie couldn't think when he was touching her so intimately. She'd dreamt of this moment for so long and it was overwhelming now to be experiencing it. The words came out. She couldn't stop them. 'I want you, Nic...so much. I've always wanted you...'

His hand stilled for a moment. Maddie couldn't fathom the cynical look that crossed Nic's face.

'You'll say anything, won't you?'

She shook her head, nearly crying out when his hand and fingers started moving again, harder this time, as if he was angry and sensed her hunger. 'I don't—'

She gasped when she felt him slide one finger inside her panties, close to where the secret folds of her body hid the full extent of her desire and vulnerability.

'Yes...you do. But it doesn't matter any more. Nothing matters except this.'

And with a guttural growl he bent his head, his mouth finding hers in a drugging heady kiss while one finger thrust deep inside her damp heat, making her scream into his mouth. Now she was utterly exposed and undone. There was no going back, only forward.

Maddie was barely aware of her hands ripping at Nic's shirt. She only knew that she craved to see his chest, to feel it next to hers, rubbing against her breasts. And all the while his hand was between her legs, which were splayed outwards. One finger became two and Maddie nearly passed out. The pleasure was so intense.

And then he was tugging her panties down, taking his hand away for a moment, putting her legs together to undress her. Maddie felt feverish now. Hot all over.

His shirt was swinging open, his chest broad and tautly muscled. A smattering of dark golden hair covered his pectoral muscles and arrowed down to his pants in a tantalising and utterly masculine line. He sat back for a moment and she saw his hands come to his belt. With wide eyes she lay back and watched as he opened his pants, tore down his zip and yanked them down. His briefs were tented over a long and thick bulge. Maddie could feel nothing but intense excitement.

She vaguely heard foil ripping, and saw Nic's erection spring free as he ripped down his briefs. He rolled on a condom and came back over her, spreading her legs again to accommodate him as easily as if she were a pliable doll. Maddie was vaguely aware that her dress was bunched up around her waist and pulled down under her breasts. She didn't care.

Nic's hand was between her legs again and she cried out at the contact, her chest coming up into contact with Nic's. 'Please,' she sobbed. 'Please...do something.'

She didn't even know what to ask for. All she knew was that she needed *more*.

Nic shifted his weight onto his hands and Maddie's legs fell open wider. She could feel the thick blunt head of his penis as he started to push into her. Her muscles contracted at the alien invasion and her eyes grew wide. She knew she wanted this, needed it, but a sudden instinct that pain was inevitable seized her muscles.

Nic sank in some more, and pain hit like a steam train crashing into her chest. Maddie sucked in a shocked breath. The pain was white-hot.

Nic frowned and cursed softly. 'You're so tight…'

Instinctively, as if Maddie knew that the only way was to go through it, she arched up, forcing Nic to impale her a little more. She cried out at the shocking, rending pain. But her hands were on his buttocks and a fierce determination gripped her.

She looked up into Nic's eyes and saw the dawning understanding. '*Dios*, Maddie…you're not…?'

'Don't say it,' she said fiercely, feeling sweat break out on her brow. 'Don't you dare stop now.'

For a long moment tension gripped them both. The broad head of Nic's shaft was barely inside her and the pain was clearly devastating, but all he could see was her flushed cheeks and that stark determination in her eyes. So many things were hitting him at once, but the biggest one was a feeling of exhilaration. She was *his*. She would become his right now and no one else's.

He thought she'd been playing a part even when she'd told him how much she wanted him. This revelation smashed that assertion to pieces and left Nic spinning off in a direction he couldn't even begin to look at now.

Nic found some control from somewhere and gritted out painfully, 'This is going to hurt…but it won't last, I promise.'

Maddie looked up at him, tousled and flushed and beautiful. She bit her lip and said, 'Okay.'

The trust in her eyes nearly broke him in two, and with

sweat forming tiny beads on his chest Nic gritted his jaw and drove himself into her reluctant flesh. She cried out. Her hands gripped his buttocks fiercely and Nic nearly came right then at the feel of her body clamping so tightly around his.

She was crying in earnest, tears trickling out of her eyes, but still she was not pushing him away. Nic felt weak at her show of bravery. He put his forehead to hers and then pressed a kiss to her mouth. He could taste her salty tears and crooned softly, 'It's okay, *querida*, that's the worst bit...just try to relax...let me move and it'll feel better... I promise.'

Maddie felt light-headed from the pain, but there was something deep within her melting and reacting to Nic's tender words. Something that she'd shut away long ago coming to life again. She felt like a warrior. She wanted to embrace the pain with this man. She pressed a kiss to his shoulder, as if to tell him she trusted him. She couldn't speak.

Slowly she could feel her flesh adapting to his, relaxing ever so slightly from its tight grip around him. He sank in a little more—unbelievably. Eventually she could feel his pelvis snug against hers. And it didn't hurt as much. The pain was being replaced with sensations. Flutterings along nerve-ends.

Slowly Nic started to withdraw, and instinctively Maddie clutched at his tight buttocks as if to stop him. He pressed a kiss to her mouth, which felt swollen and bruised. 'No, sweetheart...trust me...let me go.'

Maddie relaxed her hold and he continued to slide out, so slowly that little exquisite shards of sensation started to flutter through her lower body. When he was almost entirely out he drove in again, and this time his passage was smoother, increasing those flutters.

Maddie's hips moved. She rolled them, forcing Nic to curse and say, 'Stop, Maddie...this is hard enough...I won't last...'

She stopped, in awe of his strength and size, and the extreme gentleness he was showing her. She tried to stay as still as possible as he taught her flesh and her body how to respond to him, but an urgency was building, the pain was being washed away by pleasure. A kind of pleasure she'd never felt before.

Digging her heels into the soft, fragrant earth beside his thighs, Maddie couldn't stop herself from moving—just as Nic's own movements became faster and more urgent. Blood was thundering through her body. Her heart hammered. She was straining, searching for something but she didn't know what.

She felt Nic put a hand between them—right there, near where he was driving in and out with relentless precision. Each thrust getting harder and faster and deeper.

Maddie wrapped her legs around his slim hips, deepening the penetration even more, just as his thumb found her sensitised clitoris and stroked it. Pleasure exploded with unstoppable force inside Maddie's whole body, radiating outwards from that thumb and his own driving flesh. It was like an endless wave, so breathtaking in its magnitude that Maddie was incoherent, bucking wildly beneath Nic as he ground himself into her and shouted out.

His whole body went taut for a long moment, every sinew and muscle locked. She could feel him pulsing and throbbing inside her, and then he was spent, and his whole weight came crashing down, crushing her to the ground.

Maddie wrapped her arms around him and knew in that moment that she loved Nic de Rojas. She'd never hated him. She couldn't. She'd fallen for him from a distance as a lovestruck teenager, and that had become a solid reality when she'd stood before him in this place all those years ago. Now...after giving herself to him completely...it was cemented deep in her cells for ever. And he would break her heart into tiny pieces even as he showed her paradise.

Maddie was barely aware of their journey home along the trail, lit now by moonlight. She was only aware that she was sitting within the cradle of Nic's strong hard thighs on his horse while he held the reins of her own, leading it home.

One arm was clamped around her waist, and she couldn't stop her head from sinking back into his chest as extreme lethargy washed through every bone and cell in her body.

Having Maddie sitting so close to where Nic still ached was a form of torture so delicious he never wanted it to end. His brain was reeling from an overload of pleasure more intense than anything he'd ever experienced or could have imagined. Even the memory of thrusting into Maddie's tight embrace had his libido raging again, and he had to grit his teeth to counteract it.

So many thoughts were vying for dominance. But one superceded them all. *She'd been a virgin.* She hadn't slept with Morales. Even though deep down Nic had believed her, there'd been a tiny part of him unwilling to give up a kernel of doubt. As if the minute he trusted her she'd laugh in his face.

She'd given herself to him more passionately and unself-consciously than the most experienced woman he'd ever bedded. He'd never forget that blazing look of trust when she'd been in such pain but had not shied away from it. She'd embraced it like a pagan warrior.

He'd only become aware afterwards that he'd still been half dressed. His trousers had been around his ankles and he'd bunched her dress around her waist. He'd been like an animal in heat.

Everything was spinning out of Nic's control. His chest felt too full. And yet he couldn't stop his arm from tightening around her even more, or the exultation that whispered through him when her soft breath sighed over his skin.

Maddie only came to again when she sensed she was being carried in Nic's arms through the quiet house. She could barely lift her head. That delicious lethargy was weighing everything down, including her mind, where dangerous thoughts hovered. Everything was still and hushed and quiet.

Maddie looked up to see the stark planes of Nic's face above her. Without thinking about what she was doing, she reached up and cupped his strong jaw. She could feel him grit it against her hand.

Then she heard a door hit a wall, and she was being carried into a dimly lit and unashamedly masculine room. Nic's bedroom. Once again sanity hovered on the edge of her consciousness, but Maddie was a coward. It was as if they were in a bubble and she couldn't bear for the bubble to burst yet.

Nic put her down gently on the side of the bed and Maddie winced when sensitive flesh came in contact with the soft surface.

Immediately Nic was crouching at face level. 'Are you sore?'

Maddie felt inexplicably shy and blushed. 'A little… but it's fine.'

Just looking at him now was making blood rush back to all her extremities. Making her *want* all over again.

Nic pressed a swift kiss to her mouth, and then said, 'Give me one minute and I'll make you feel better.'

She watched speechlessly as he stood up and strode towards the bathroom. She only noticed then that she had all but ripped his shirt off like some demented madwoman. Her heart swelled in her chest, and once again she blocked those dangerous tendrils of reality from intruding.

Nic was back and coming towards her, stripping off his ruined shirt, revealing that huge expanse of glorious, hard-muscled chest. Maddie's insides clenched down low. Lord, he was even more beautiful than she'd thought.

He reached for her and, as if she was full of magnets aligning themselves only to him, she was effortlessly swept into his arms. She curled up tight against his chest, relishing the profound sense of protection in his embrace.

Steam was building up in the bathroom and Maddie could hear the shower running. Gently Nic let her down, and she found her legs to be ridiculously wobbly. They got even worse when he pulled her zip down and tried to pull down her grass-stained dress over her breasts. Instinctively Maddie's hands came up. She looked up into wry blue eyes.

'Don't you think it's a little late for modesty?'

Maddie tried to smile but it felt brittle. Slowly Nic took her hands away and peeled the dress down. Maddie's cheeks flamed. His eyes devoured her hungrily and she watched as he lifted his hands to cup the full mounds of pale flesh. She bit her lip when she felt her nipples responding, growing tight with need again.

In an instant Nic's hands had dropped and he stepped away, saying gutturally, 'I can't stop touching you...'

Acting on instinct, Maddie stepped forward and lifted his hands to cup her flesh again. 'I like it... Don't stop.'

His eyes met hers, and they were blazing. She could feel his hands tremble slightly and a wave of tenderness washed over her.

Nic spoke abruptly, taking his hands away. 'No...if I start now...

'I won't have you on the floor of the bathroom.'

He quickly dispensed with her dress and his own clothes, and then led her into the huge shower stall and under the powerful spray. Maddie let her head drop back as the water cascaded down, and murmured luxuriously when she felt Nic's soapy hands running all over her.

By the time he was done she was leaning weakly against the wall of the shower and begging him to stop.

With stark need stamped on his face he handed her the soap and said, 'Your turn.'

Lord.

Maddie took the soap and lathered up. Nic rested his hands high, either side of her head, so that he formed a cage around her, and gave her his body. As Maddie smoothed soapy hands over his shoulders and down his chest her eyes grew wide. And when she got lower and saw the proud jutting swell of his erection they got wider. Fascinated, she wrapped one slick soapy hand around him and exulted in his sharply indrawn breath. He was all silky skin encasing pure steel.

As much to distract herself as anything else, she ordered him to turn around and he muttered, 'Spoilsport.'

Maddie faced his back and lifted her hands, but they stilled in horror when she saw the lurid white lines slashing across his powerful muscles. They extended from his neck down to his waist.

As if he'd just realised what she was looking at, he whipped around so fast her head spun.

She felt sick as she looked up into his white face. 'What are those marks?'

He just looked at her for a long moment and said nothing, but he reached for the control and switched the shower off. He stepped out and hitched a towel around his waist, handed her one. She took it wordlessly, a chill skating over her skin.

She stepped out and briskly rubbed her hair, before putting the towel around her own body and following him into his room. He was standing at his window, arms folded, looking outwards. Maddie stopped uncertainly. This was completely uncharted territory.

'Nic?'

She could see his muscles tense even more, and those scars stood out in vivid relief. She had a flashback to that moment eight years before, when his father's men had had to beat him to get him to come with them, and dread turned her blood to ice. She forced her legs to move and stood in front of him. She looked up.

'It happened that day, didn't it? Those men...they beat you?'

Nic was looking resolutely above Maddie's head and his jaw was clenched. Her heart ached.

'What do you care?' he asked coolly.

All signs of passion were gone. Rejection emanated from every tense line in his body. He'd never been more remote. Exactly as he had been that day when she'd gone back and seen him...and hadn't been able to hide her horror.

Maddie was in turmoil. 'I just...I want to know what happened...'

He looked down at her then, and his eyes were like two ice chips. She shivered.

He raised a brow. 'You *really* want to know the sordid details?'

CHAPTER NINE

MADDIE nodded even as her heart thumped. They couldn't be any more sordid than what she'd been through in the aftermath of that cataclysmic afternoon.

Nic's voice was devoid of any expression. 'My father's men brought me back to the house, where they informed him of who I'd been found with and what we'd been doing. My father was angrier than I've ever seen him. He brought me out to the yard in the middle of the stables and ordered the men to hold me down so he could whip me.'

Maddie just looked at Nic. All she could see in her mind's eye was his face when she'd seen him the following day…before he'd turned so icy and cruel. He'd been pale. He must have been in agony, yet he'd come back… to see her. Perhaps he hadn't meant those cruel words he'd uttered? Perhaps he'd just been protecting himself against her extreme reaction.

The revelation made Maddie feel weak inside even as Nic continued in that toneless voice, 'With the benefit of hindsight I can see how making love to his own ex-lover's daughter must have pushed a button or two, though I didn't know that then.'

Maddie started to tremble violently, unable to expunge from her mind the horrific image of him being whipped.

And all because of what they'd done so innocently. The ripples had been catastrophic.

Nic caught her expression. 'You don't have to put on a horrified act, Maddie. I would have thought you'd appreciate the melodrama our actions inspired. Isn't that what you were looking for to alleviate your boredom?'

Melodrama! Boredom! Maddie nearly cried out loud. He had no idea. He'd been horsewhipped. Because of *her*. Maddie couldn't stop her emotions from boiling over. She put a hand over her mouth and fled for the bathroom, just making it to the toilet in time, where she retched over the toilet bowl.

She felt his presence behind her and begged weakly, 'Just leave me alone. Please.'

His voice sounded tight. 'No. Let me help...'

Before Maddie could protest she was being lifted up and a cool wet cloth was being pressed to her face. Nic handed her some toothpaste on a brush and she brushed her teeth. When she was done he took her hand and led her back to the bedroom. Maddie pulled her hand free from his and sat on the edge of the bed.

Nic stood apart and looked down at her, his expression guarded. 'You're an enigma, Madalena Vasquez. You set out to tease me years ago, and when I tell you what happened to me it makes you physically ill.'

His jaw clenched then, as if he was remembering something, and Maddie could see him start to retreat. She knew exactly what he was remembering: her cruel words. She desperately wanted to erase them for ever.

Huskily she said, 'I never set out to tease you, Nic, or to humiliate you. I promise on my father's life I had no plan, no agenda. When you followed me that first day I was terrified—but exhilarated. I wanted you...but I would never have set out to seduce you just for fun.' Her voice grew husky. 'That week… It meant something to me.'

Nic reached out and caught her arms in his hands, pulled her up to face him. He bit out through a clenched jaw, 'Don't try and rewrite history, Maddie. You seduced me because you were bored. That week was a diversion— nothing more.'

Maddie shook her head. 'No,' she whispered. 'It wasn't. I *wanted* to see you again.'

She felt herself teetering on the edge of a precipice. At the last moment she knew she couldn't tell him everything, so she'd furnish him with half a truth. She took a shaky breath. 'When we were discovered that day and I was taken home, my mother was livid. We had a huge fight and she told me about the affair she'd had with your father… My father overheard…'

Maddie comforted herself that what she was saying wasn't a complete fabrication; she was just ommitting certain information.

She went on, 'When I saw you the next day I couldn't tell you about the affair. It was too sordid. I was ashamed, and I was afraid of what would happen if they thought I was still seeing you. I had to make you leave, so I said the most hurtful things I could think of, but they weren't true…'

Maddie felt more exposed than she'd ever felt. She'd just revealed her heart to him. She looked away, terrified he'd see the emotion, see the lie in her eyes. What she *wasn't* telling him. The darker truth.

He released her and tipped up her chin, spearing her with that laser like gaze. 'Before your father came a few weeks after that, and my mother and I found out about the affair, I'd always assumed you and your mother left so quickly because you wanted to get away from here—and *me.*'

Maddie shook her head, her heart aching at the thought of how Nic had interpreted events. She suddenly felt sick again. Maybe Nic already *knew* the awful thing she'd carried with her for so long?

Hesitantly she asked, 'What did my father say to your parents, exactly?'

Nic stepped back, raking a hand through his hair impatiently. His whole body radiated tension. 'It was my mother he wanted to speak to.' He smiled bitterly. 'After all, my father already knew. My father was away that day. I just remember finding her hysterical, ranting about your mother and my father together. I had to get the doctor and he sedated her. A couple of days later she took an overdose of pills and left a note telling my father that she knew everything. It was bad enough having found *us* together, but after my mother's suicide the old enmity was truly alive and well again. Father's rage eventually led to his own heart attack...'

Maddie's stomach churned. It didn't sound as if his mother had elaborated on *everything.* If her father *had* told Nic's mother the full ugly truth she must have taken the information to her grave. Maybe it had been too horrific to comprehend. There was no way Nic's father wouldn't have used that information for his own ends to get back at her father or his son, she suspected, if he'd known.

Maddie couldn't help herself from reaching out to touch Nic's arm. 'I'm so sorry.'

Nic smiled, but it was tight and bitter. 'My mother wasn't exactly stable at the best of times. She most likely suffered from something clinical, like bipolar disorder, but it was never diagnosed. It didn't take much to push her over the edge.'

Maddie felt as if she was treading on eggshells. 'It must have been hard growing up with that...inconsistency.'

Nic emitted a curt laugh and pulled back from Maddie's touch. Her hand dropped ineffectually.

'You could say that. If Father wasn't trying to toughen up his runt of a son, Mother was weeping silently in a corner.'

Maddie's heart clenched at hearing Nic refer to his physical weakness again. Galvanised by something she couldn't name, Maddie said with a touch of defiance, 'Yet you overcame it and proved him wrong...'

Something bleak crossed Nic's face. 'Even then he couldn't respect me. I think it angered him to know that I'd prevailed.' Nic's mouth twisted. 'It just meant that he had to get his men to hold me down to thrash me. He no longer had the satisfaction alone.'

Maddie felt tears spring into her eyes. She'd had no idea he'd been so brutalised by his father.

Nic must have seen the brightness in her eyes and he quickly closed the distance between them, hauling her body into his.

A huge lump was in Maddie's throat, an ache in her chest. Nic looked ferocious.

'I think it's time we stopped talking and remembered what this evening is about...'

Nic's mouth was on Maddie's before she could respond. Tears were running down her face, but he was ruthless, intent on sucking her back under to a place where no words were needed. Maddie eventually gave in, her arms snaking around Nic's neck and the ache in her heart intensifying even as the tears eventually dried on her cheeks and her sobs of emotion became sobs of need and want under Nic's masterful touch.

* * *

When Maddie woke the following morning it took a long time for her to register where she was and what had happened. Her body ached, but pleasurably. Between her legs she was tender and slightly sore.

Maddie groaned. It all came back. The dress; the dinner; the orchard…and back here in Nic's room. She opened her eyes wider and looked around. She wasn't in Nic's room, in his bed any more. Even though dawn had been breaking outside when she'd finally fallen asleep.

He must have brought her back here, to the room she'd been shown into yesterday evening. Immediately Maddie felt vulnerable at the thought of Nic depositing her here while she slept, as if he was done with her. As if he couldn't bear to be with her for a moment longer. And with sick realization, Maddie knew why. He had to resent her for making him open up, for telling her what he had. He'd been through so much. The thought of him returning to the orchard that last day with his back ripped apart from a whip made her want to cry all over again.

A knock sounded on the door, making her flinch. Maddie squeaked something, half terrified it might be Nic—she wasn't ready to see him. Not when she was feeling so emotional. But it was the same girl who'd shown her to the dining room the previous evening. Relief flooded Maddie when she came in with a breakfast tray.

Maddie sat up, acutely self-conscious of her nakedness under the sheet. The girl put the tray on a table and then said shyly, 'I have a message from Mr de Rojas—he says that he will see you at your home this afternoon.'

The contract.

Maddie felt a hard ball lodge in her belly. She thanked the girl and when she'd left got shakily out of the bed, wrapping a towel around her. She went to the window and looked out. The view took in the eastern slopes of Nic's vineyard, with the snow-capped Andes mountains in the distance. It was stunning.

And then she saw him, striding down a row of vines in the distance. She shrank back, even though there was no way he could see her from where he was. But in that moment he looked up in her direction. Maddie ducked, her heart beating furiously. Humiliation burnt her up inside as she huddled there pathetically.

He couldn't even be bothered to come and tell her himself. The night was over. He'd got what he wanted, which was to see her as exposed and rejected as she had made him feel all those years before. If he had felt anything for her once, it was long gone.

Nic cursed himself for looking up at Maddie's bedroom window, and for fancying for a second that he might have seen her. She'd been dead to the world when he'd left her in the bed, her pale skin marked and lightly bruised from where he'd gripped her in the throes of passion.

Even now his blood rushed south, hardening his body, and he cursed out loud. He ripped a grape off the vine and bit into it, wincing slightly. Eduardo, his head winemaker, was looking at him, and Nic suddenly needed to be alone.

He said curtly, 'Another couple of days before we pick these. I'll find you later to check the others.'

Eduardo took the hint and nodded, walking away, and Nic breathed out a sigh of relief. His head was so tangled and snarled up since last night. Maddie was the first woman he'd fallen asleep with, whose touch he'd instinctively sought, wrapping his body around hers as if loath to let her go. *That* more than anything else had galvanised him into bringing her back to her own room to put some space between them.

He hungered for her even more acutely now that he'd

tasted every bit of her. Another first. Usually his desire was dented very quickly.

Last night had veered off the tracks in a big way the moment Maddie had stood up from the dinner table and started taking off the jewellery and shoes. And then...the orchard. Even now Nic could remember the panic he'd felt when he'd realised that was her intention. And yet at the same time something had resonated deep inside him—a need to get out of the falsely polite structure he'd insisted on with the dinner.

When he'd seen her standing among those trees it had felt terrifying, but completely right. As if there could be no other place for them to seek closure, no matter how exposed it made him feel. But all of that had fallen away as soon as he'd started kissing her. And when he'd discovered her innocence...

Nic's insides turned molten even now. She'd been a virgin. She was his and no one else's.

Nic hadn't even realised his hand was full of grapes until he felt the sticky juice oozing between his fingers. He looked at his hand and saw that it was trembling slightly. He recalled the tears in Maddie's eyes when he'd told her about his parents. That effortless feeling of affinity she'd evoked. Exactly as she had once before...

Past and present were meshing dangerously.

Sleeping with Maddie last night should have been a clinical exercise, and it had been anything but. It had morphed into something completely different. It proved to him how dangerous she was—how easily she slipped under his guard and elicited information from him. Exactly as she'd done before.

Even what she'd told him about *her* version of events that week was too huge for him to digest right now. It put a spin on things that threatened everything.

For a moment Nic felt panic steal over him—a completely alien emotion. And then he remembered the contract. Relief flooded him. The contract put a boundary around last night and around *him*. And more importantly it put a boundary around Maddie, keeping her at a distance from Nic.

Maddie was operating at a level of numbness which was working very well for her. She was blocking out the previous night's events, and if some lurid images snuck through her ironclad defences she closed her eyes and meditated on something else until they disappeared.

It was lonely in the house without Hernan and Maria. She'd spoken to Hernan on the phone earlier and had been devastated to learn that Maria would need an operation. Maddie had told Hernan to stay with Maria for as long as he needed. They were hoping that the operation would take place the following week.

Feeling restless, and not looking forward to a visit from a triumphant Nic with the contract, Maddie set out to check the cellars. She needed to start making an inventory of the things she needed. No doubt Nic would expect her to be well prepared for when his funds became available now that they'd be on a purely business footing.

Maddie felt no great sense of excitement that her estate was going to receive an injection of funds. It all felt flat now, meaningless.

When she remembered how she'd felt in Nic's arms last night in the orchard—the wave of love that had come over her—she assured herself that it was just because he'd been her first lover. Heightened emotion.

Maddie resolutely forced Nic from her mind yet again, and concentrated on making notes. More time had passed than she'd realised when she noticed that she was stiff from bending over and squinting at barrel labels. She'd been hoping that she might find a hidden gem of a barrel full of untouched wine, but no such luck.

Then she heard a distinctly bad-tempered-sounding *'Maddie!'*

For a perverse moment Maddie considered hiding among the barrels, as she and her brother had used to do when they'd been small, but she squared her shoulders and called out, 'Down here.'

She heard him before she saw him, and already her skin was tingling and she was remembering—and biting her lip trying *not* to remember. And then he appeared, in a loose shirt and jeans, hair dishevelled, looking so gorgeous that her lower body instantly grew hot and tingly.

Maddie couldn't speak, but it appeared Nic had enough to say for both of them. He strode towards her, eyes flashing with displeasure. 'How the hell does anyone know where to find you? Why don't you have a mobile phone? You could have been anywhere on the estate—'

He broke off and came closer, eyes sparking down into Maddie's, and to her utter chagrin she felt ridiculously emotional and close to tears.

'Well, I'm here, as you can see.' Maddie hated that she was so raw.

Nic seemed to temper his own response. 'I couldn't find you. I looked all over the estate... If anything happened to you—if you fell and sprained an ankle or anything...' He stopped and cursed. 'I need to know where you are.'

Maddie's treacherous heart leapt at *'I need to know where you are'*, but just as quickly she ruthlessly drove down that insidious emotion.

She stepped back and said coolly, 'Let's not pretend you're actually concerned, Nic. You just don't have time to spend looking for a business associate. Did you bring the contract?'

Nic seemed to blanch before her eyes, but then colour rushed swiftly back. His response surprised her, but he seemed to control himself. 'Yes, I did. It's upstairs in your father's study.'

Nic let Maddie precede him out of the cellar, and used the opportunity to get himself back under control. All of his earlier assurances had died a quick death when he'd come to the estate and hadn't been able to find any trace of Maddie anywhere. Panic had escalated as he'd imagined her lying somewhere, helpless. With so much out-of-date machinery in this place anything was possible.

And then, when he had found her, the relief had been overwhelming.

By the time he was following her into her father's study Nic was firmly back in control. He watched as Maddie sat down and pulled the contract towards her. She scanned it briefly and looked up at him with that cool expression on her face. It made Nic's blood boil and his loins ache. He wanted to see her undone again. Right now.

'Hernan won't be back for a few days. I'll have to wait till he gets here to go over this.'

Nic saw Maddie's throat work, the slight pink colour suffusing her skin. *Good.* She wasn't as cool as she looked, after all.

Nic dragged his attention from Maddie's physical response. 'I heard about Maria earlier. She's receiving the best of care, and the physician is confident it's a routine enough operation. He doesn't envisage any complications.'

Maddie said carefully, 'That's good… But this will have to wait until Hernan is back. I can't bother him with it now.'

Nic felt something like relief flow through his system.

A reprieve. He suddenly hated that damn contract. He conveniently pushed aside the memory of the panic he'd felt that morning. All he wanted was Maddie.

Maddie did not like the look on Nic's face as he prowled closer to the heavy oak desk. He put his hands down on top of it and said throatily, 'That's absolutely fine with me. But until the agreement is signed this isn't over.'

Maddie gulped, all pretence of insouciance fleeing. 'What isn't over?'

Nic came around the table and tugged Maddie out of the chair so she was standing flush against his body.

'This.'

And he wrapped his arms around her and pulled her so tightly into him that her curves melded into his hard muscles like the pieces of a jigsaw. Maddie made her hands into fists and hit out ineffectually, but Nic's mouth was on her jaw and trailing hot kisses down her neck to where the pulse was thumping out of her skin.

She groaned weakly. 'Nic...*no.*'

Nic's answer was to bend and lift her into his arms, making her squeal. He looked at her. 'Where's your room?'

Maddie was torn, already breathing heavily, her whole body aching for this man's touch. She knew a thousand and one reasons why she shouldn't do this, and yet the moment seemed fragile and illusory, as if it was a dream. There was a lightness between them for the first time.

'Upstairs, second door on the right.'

Nic's face was grim, but the heat in his eyes mesmerised Maddie. She hated herself for being so weak.

When Nic brought her into the sparsely furnished room with its plain double bed everything seemed to fall away. Past, present and future. There was only now, and this crazy, unexpected reprieve. She could recognise now that she was relieved that she hadn't signed the contract yet. Until she did she was a free woman—not beholden to Nic de Rojas.

Nic was opening the buttons on her shirt, and Maddie lifted her hands to do the same to his. Nic pushed her shirt off her shoulders and down her arms. His went the same way. Nic reached around and tugged Maddie's hair free of its band, so that it fell around her shoulders. In an endearingly gentle moment he spread his fingers through the silky strands of her hair, hands cupping her head, massaging it gently. He tipped her face up to his and something inside Maddie quivered ominously.

'This isn't over...not yet...'

And then Nic was kissing her, drugging her. With deft hands he unfastened her bra, letting it follow their shirts to the floor. Then he was cupping both breasts in his hands, massaging their firmness, trapping her nipples in his fingers, making Maddie moan into his mouth.

He took his mouth from hers and lifted one voluptuous breast so that he could swirl his tongue around the hard tip. His arm had come around her back, supporting her, arching her into him. Maddie's hands were in Nic's hair, mussing it up.

When he deposited her on the bed and opened her jeans she lifted her hips to help him. Her knickers disappeared too, but Maddie didn't have time to be embarrassed. She was too hot, waiting impatiently for Nic to finish taking off his own clothes, revealing his impressively taut body.

Maddie breathed in, sighing with deep-seated pleasure when Nic came down beside her. One hand pushed her thighs apart so that he could stroke with his fingers where she ached most.

Maddie couldn't have articulated a coherent thought

even if she'd wanted to. By the time Nic had donned protection and was pushing into her hot moist core, Maddie knew she would take this for as long as it lasted. And deal with the fallout later.

When Maddie woke much later it was dark outside. She was alone in the bed, and instantly cold when she recalled what had happened. Within minutes of seeing Nic again they'd been in bed. That had *never* been a part of the plan. It was meant to be one night and then she'd sign the contract…except she remembered now that she hadn't signed it. Guilty relief curled through her. It was as if they could ignore the inevitable for as long as the contract didn't exist. But Maddie knew that as soon as it was signed everything would change.

She tensed when she heard a faint noise from downstairs. The kitchen was two floors below her room, but the sounds sometimes carried up. She got out of bed and pulled on her jeans and shirt, smoothing her hair as best she could.

Creeping downstairs, she heard tuneless whistling as she got closer to the kitchen. She stopped at the door and her jaw dropped at the sight before her. Nic was in his shirt, which was buttoned up wrong, and the low-slung jeans with the top button still open, deftly tossing pancakes. His jaw was dark with stubble.

He spotted her and stopped whistling. 'How do you like yours?' he asked. 'With cream or chocolate or strawberries?'

Maddie went in and felt as if she was in some kind of twilight zone. Faintly she said, 'Where did you get all this stuff?'

Nic answered easily. 'I went out.'

Maddie looked at him, aghast. 'What time is it? How long was I asleep?'

Nic consulted his watch. 'It's nine p.m. and you were out for about four hours.'

Maddie blanched. 'You should have woken me.' She looked away, not wanting him to read in her expression or her eyes that she was relieved to see him still here.

Lightly he said, 'You looked far too peaceful.'

What Nic was thinking was that he didn't like how much he wanted to see the delicate purplish signs of fatigue gone from under Maddie's eyes. When he'd woken it had taken all of his restraint not to wake her with a kiss, or pull her back into his hardening body.

He'd come downstairs, and when he'd seen the pitiful state of affairs in the kitchen guilt had swamped him. He'd gone shopping for the first time in years. And as he'd shopped Nic had realised that for the first time in a long time he felt unaccountably lighter.

Without the contract between them Nic had seen a barrier being removed. They could continue this affair... because surely after another couple of nights he'd get that familiar sense of ennui and be able to move on from her?

Nic's jaw clenched now as he acknowledged that if anything his hunger for Maddie was only sharper. He could smell their mingled scent in the air and it was like the headiest of perfumes. Suddenly he wanted to swipe all the ingredients and shopping off the counter and take Maddie there and then.

Maddie sat down gingerly on a stool and watched Nic prepare another pancake. He'd already prepared about six. Half jokingly she said, 'How many are coming to dinner?'

He looked up, and Maddie felt speared by the intensity of his gaze. He smiled a crooked smile. 'I used to make tons of these when I worked in the vineyards in France during a European summer. We had to take it in turns to cook…communal living,' he explained. 'I was doing my Master of Wine course.'

Maddie shook her head. 'That's such an achievement. Your father must have been proud of that…' When Maddie saw Nic tense she cursed herself inwardly. But he spoke after a moment.

'He died just after I got my results. He didn't appear to be impressed.'

Maddie felt exposed at this acknowledgement of the lack of love he'd faced from his own father. Something that was all too familiar to her.

'So, have you made your mind up yet?'

She saw him hold up a jar of chocolate spread in one hand and a carton of cream in the other. To Maddie's intense shock, because she'd never thought of herself as an erotically minded person, she immediately had a vision of Nic putting some chocolate spread on her nipple and then licking it off.

Cheeks flaming, she blurted out, 'Cream and strawberries. Please.'

Nic just looked at her with a knowing glint in his eye and put the chocolate down, saying, 'Maybe you'll try that one later.'

Completely mortified, Maddie said nothing, and waited for Nic to serve her a pancake oozing with cream and strawberries. He handed her a glass of sparkling clear wine and Maddie took a sip, letting the effervescence take her far, far away from the reality that this was very finite and all too transitory.

'Nic, what is this? What are we doing?'

Nic closed his eyes momentarily, as if that might help block out the memory of Maddie's husky voice a short while before. He'd just pulled on his jeans and shirt and turned around to see Maddie resting back on her elbows in the bed, looking deliciously tousled and flushed. The sheet had barely hidden the curves of her breasts and inevitably, even though so recently sated, his body had started to hum with energy and renewed desire.

Who was he kidding? Here in his Jeep, driving away, it was still humming.

Three days had passed now. Three days and heady nights when time had seemed to blur and lose focus as soon as Nic drove into the gates of the Vasquez estate. He had gone there each day, ostensibly to talk to Maddie about what she wanted to do with the vineyard, but as soon as he saw her they inevitably ended up in bed. The desire between them was insatiable.

Damn, damn, damn, damn. Nic hit his fist off the steering wheel.

Maddie was under his skin, in his blood. In the very place he'd wanted to keep her out, and in a place no other woman had got close to. Since that week in the orchard, when he'd come so close to allowing himself to be emotionally vulnerable for the first time in his life, he'd kept his heart closed off to everyone around him. He'd learnt his lesson and he'd learnt it well.

Despite that, Nic knew he had to revise his whole memory of what had happened eight years ago. Maddie had been innocent—not even aware of her own power. Yet her words still stung. The vehemence with which she'd uttered them was still vivid and the way she'd been physically sick when he'd touched her. But he had to concede now that perhaps it had just been overwrought teenage dramatics in the aftermath of hearing the bombshell news of her mother's affair.

Her words resounded in his head again like a taunt: *'Nic, what is this? What are we doing?'*

He'd gone back over to Maddie in the bed and taken her face in his hands, pressing a long, lingering kiss to her mouth. When his heart had begun thundering and he'd known he was fast hurtling towards the point of no return he'd pulled back and said, 'Until the contract is signed, *this* is what we're doing.'

She'd stiffened and pulled at the sheet, forcing Nic to stand up.

'And then it's over—just like that?'

Nic had looked down into those wide green eyes and seen something that had made him profoundly nervous. It was a reflection of himself as a younger man, laying himself bare for ridicule. He couldn't go back there—not for anyone.

He'd spoken past a huge constriction in his chest. 'It can't be anything else...not if you want this investment.'

Maddie had paled, but then she'd looked him dead in the eye. 'I just wanted to be sure there was no confusion.'

Suddenly Nic had felt anger rise at her coolness. He'd bent and pressed another kiss to her mouth, only satisfied when she gave a helpless little mewling sound revealing her lack of control.

He'd stood back from the bed. 'I'll be back later, to go over some business details with you.'

With defiance evident in her voice, Maddie had said, 'I'm going into the clinic to see Maria this afternoon. Her operation has been brought forward to tomorrow.'

'Well, then,' Nic had gritted out, 'I'll come and get you and we can go together—after we've discussed business.'

Nic was well aware that once Maria's operation was over and she was in recovery, Hernan would come back to

Villarosa and look over the contract. And Maddie would sign. And this edgy truce between them would be over.

Because Madalena Vasquez was linked to too many emotions and memories for it to become anything else.

CHAPTER TEN

MADDIE felt a vibrating in her jeans pocket, took out the mobile phone Nic had given her, and scowled at it before answering.

All she heard was an autocratic, 'Where are you?' and instantly her insides were melting and blood was rushing to the sensitive parts of her body.

She gritted her jaw. 'I'm at the vats.'

She ended the connection, feeling very shaky. She had been ever since that morning, when Nic had laid it out so baldly—that this affair would last only until the contract was signed and then return to a platonic business relationship. It should be making her feel happy. Surely she wasn't naive enough to think it could be anything else?

Maddie knew that for her own sanity she should be grateful. There was too much history between them. The feud might not exist any more but it had wreaked too much havoc to be healed by them alone...

She sighed now, and nearly jumped out of her skin when she heard a soft, 'Don't fall in.'

Maddie whirled around to see Nic on the catwalk. She'd been so engrossed that she hadn't even heard his Jeep, or his arrival on the steel catwalk. She turned away, scared he'd see how raw she felt. 'I did fall in once...when I was about nine.'

She heard Nic gasp audibly. 'How on earth did that happen?'

Maddie smiled wryly. 'I was playing hide-and-seek with Alvaro, my brother. Hernan was here, helping with the hand-plunging. I was fascinated and leant over too far to have a look...and fell in. Luckily Hernan fished me out again straight away.'

Maddie touched her head and looked at Nic with a wry smile. 'He managed to catch my hair...I was more upset by the pain than by the fact that I could have drowned in fermenting red wine.' She dropped her hand. 'Hernan brought me home and he and Maria cleaned me up. They never told my parents...' Maddie shuddered lightly. 'If they had, my father would have locked me in my room for a week with no food.'

Nic's voice was tight. 'Did he do that a lot?'

Maddie shrugged and picked at some flaking pieces on the huge and now empty vat. 'Sometimes...if something angered him. It was more frequent after Alvaro died. He was an angry man...angry that he had a useless daughter who he couldn't pass his legacy on to.'

Suddenly conscious that she'd been babbling, Maddie changed the subject abruptly. 'These vats are in need of serious upgrading. Father got them in because he wanted to go back to concrete tanks.'

Maddie looked at Nic when he didn't say anything straight away. Then, to her relief, he said, 'We can get rid of them if you like and go back to steel. It depends on which you think is best...'

Maddie followed Nic back down to ground level and they spent the next hour discussing the various merits of upgrading the current facilities or replacing everything with the most up-to-date modern equivalent.

By the time they were on their way to the clinic in Mendoza, Maddie was feeling far more under control.

That control became shakier, though, when she witnessed Nic's concern for Maria and his insistence that she receive the best of care. He was going out of his way for people who hadn't even been his own employees.

Maddie was largely silent on their way back to Villarosa, after leaving a worried but valiantly optimistic Hernan at his wife's bedside. She wasn't prepared when Nic asked, 'What made your father change his mind?'

Half absently she said, 'About what?'

'He threw you and your mother out, turned his back on you. So why did he suddenly leave it all to you?'

Maddie tensed in her seat and Nic looked at her. For a long moment she couldn't speak. All she could think of was that awful afternoon and the horrific things she'd learnt. Feeling bile rise, she blurted out, 'Stop the car, please…'

Nic pulled over into an empty layby that was near a local beauty spot lookout, with the Andes rising majestically in the far distance. But Maddie was oblivious. She stumbled out, feeling as if a huge weight was bearing down on her.

Nic got out too and touched her shoulder. 'Maddie, what is it?'

Maddie jerked back, her eyes wide.

Nic felt Maddie jerk back. She was so pale, and her eyes were…horrorstruck. *Déjà vu* slammed into him. She'd looked at him like that before. She'd flinched like that when he'd touched her.

She spoke thickly. 'There's something…you don't know. Something else that happened after we…after we were caught.'

She whirled around and faced out to the view. They were the only people there, and it was quiet.

Nic felt his insides constricting, growing tight. As if to ward off a blow.

Through a tight jaw he asked, 'What don't I know?'

Maddie stared unseeingly at the view. 'I don't want to tell you,' she said in a low voice.

She felt Nic put his hand on her shoulder again and pull her round to face him. He dropped his hand then, as if loath to touch her, and a sense of inevitability washed over Maddie. Perhaps she did owe him the full explanation? This would bring them full circle.

'Tell me *what*, Maddie?'

Still some part of her resisted. 'I never told you because at first I couldn't. And then…then I didn't want you to have the awful blackness of it in your head, poisoning you like it did me.'

Nic shook his head, obviously completely confused. And then he looked grim. 'Maddie, we're not leaving here until you tell me what this is about.'

Maddie looked around. She felt weak all of a sudden, and went over to sit on the low wall.

Nic's hands were in his pockets. He just looked down at her.

She started hesitantly. 'I didn't tell you everything that happened when I got back to my house…after we were caught. I did start to have a fight with my mother as I told you…she was livid.'

Nic took his hands out of his pockets and folded his arms. 'Go on.'

Maddie focused on a point in the middle distance and drew in a deep breath. 'She told me that I wasn't to see you again, and I told her that she couldn't stop me.' Maddie looked at Nic then, and said softly, 'I wanted to see you again… But then she started to tell me about the affair. I didn't know what it had to do with *us* and I tried to walk out…but then she told me something else…'

Keeping her eyes on his, Maddie relayed to Nic the full extent of what her mother had told her.

'That's why I couldn't see you again…and my father had overheard every word.'

Nic felt as if he'd been punched in the gut. He looked at Maddie stupidly. And then he felt nauseous. It burned its way up, held down only by extreme strength of will.

Maddie stood up, seeing the reaction on Nic's face. 'When we went to Buenos Aires my mother agreed to get a DNA sample from my father. He gave it to her with the proviso that she would get nothing from the divorce. I got the test done and found out that I am…*was* his daughter. But of course it was too late to tell you any of this. Too much had happened. I was still traumatised by the possibility…' Maddie stopped and swallowed painfully. 'I sent a letter to my father, but never heard from him until just before he died.'

Colour was beginning to seep back into Nic's cheeks. He uncrossed his arms and ran a hand through his hair. He couldn't look at her, and Maddie felt it like the sting of a whip.

'My God, Maddie.' Nic went and stood at the low wall and looked out over the view.

Maddie turned to face the same way. She couldn't look at Nic. She bit her lip so hard she could taste blood. 'That last day…I didn't even realise I'd headed for the orchard until I got there. That's why when I saw you I reacted the way I did. How could I have told you what my mother had put in my head? It was too horrific.'

Nic sounded grim. 'Your father must have told my mother. It has to be the reason she took such a drastic step.'

Maddie nodded. 'I suspect so, yes. And I'm sorry.'

'For God's sake, Maddie, it was hardly your fault.'

His curt tone made Maddie flinch. She'd held this knowledge in for so long, and now it was out and she'd tainted Nic's head with it too. An awful helpless shaking started in her legs and rose up, taking over her whole body.

'I'm sorry. I never wanted to tell you—I shouldn't have said anything.'

Maddie heard Nic curse, and then he was turning to her and pulling her into his arms, his hands on her back, pressing her against him, stilling the awful shaking until it was just tiny tremors racking her body. She couldn't even cry.

Nic was rubbing her back now, and her hair, soothing her as if she were a wild unbroken horse.

After a long moment he pulled away and put his hands on her shoulders. He looked her in the eye. 'I'm glad you told me.'

He kept looking at her until Maddie nodded reluctantly. Then Nic took her hand and led her back to the Jeep, putting her into the passenger seat as if she were a child, securing her seat belt. Maddie felt numb, slightly removed from everything.

A grim-faced Nic got in beside her and they drove back to Villarosa. When Maddie saw Nic take the turn for his own estate she said, 'Where are we going?'

He looked at her. 'You're coming home with me tonight.'

The inevitable heat deep within Maddie started to thaw some of the numbness. It felt as if something had shifted between them as soon as she'd uttered the heinous words. When he'd held her just now his touch had been platonic. Maybe he could never desire her again with that knowledge in his head? Even though he knew it wasn't true—it was poisonous.

They got back to Nic's house. Without a word he just took her hand and led her up to his room. Maddie felt incredibly insecure and confused. She pulled free of Nic inside his bedroom door, too many evocative memories crowding her head. 'What are we doing here?' She was ashamed of how badly she wanted him.

He came and stood right in front of her. 'We're going to exorcise those demons right now, right here,' he said.

Maddie looked at him and her heart beat fast. 'What do you mean? How?'

He cupped her face in his hands and pressed close against her, so she could feel his body hardening against hers.

'Like this.'

And then he kissed her. But this was unlike any kiss they'd shared before. It reminded Maddie of how he'd kissed her for the first time—how badly she'd wanted it after the long week of building tension. He'd been so intimidatingly sexy and yet disarmingly clumsy. Like when he'd fumbled with the buttons on her blouse before opening it, and his cheeks had flushed at seeing her breasts.

It was as if past and present interlocked. Maddie was being lowered down onto the bed and Nic loomed over her. He opened her shirt and pushed it apart, pulled down the lacy cup of her bra, forcing her breast to pout up towards him.

Maddie arched her back instinctively, silently begging him to touch her.

He looked at her steadily. 'I've never forgotten how you tasted that day…the sweetness of your skin, your breast. I could have drowned in your scent…'

Maddie ran her fingers through Nic's hair, an unstoppable tide of emotion forcing her to rise up and take his face in her hands, her mouth searching for his. Each touch and moment was imbued with echoes of the past, of the way Nic had touched her that day for the first time.

They passed the moment when they'd been stopped before, and kept going. Clothes were shed and lay in a tangled heap, on the floor or under their hot slick bodies on the bed. When Nic lay between Maddie's legs his mouth was on her breast, one big hand trailing up the outside of her body, luxuriating in her satin-smooth skin, dewed with sweat.

'Nic, please…' she begged, rolling her hips impatiently.

Shifting his big body only slightly, Nic thrust into Maddie, and her whole body stilled as she looked up at him and relished the moment when their flesh joined.

'Keep your eyes open,' Nic instructed gutturally.

Maddie couldn't take her eyes off him as he slowly started to thrust in and out, taking them higher and higher and further away from the ugliness of what had happened.

When Maddie's orgasm broke over her it felt transcendental, spiritual. As if it was washing something away. Nic's gaze was searing her alive, burning into her as his own body crescendoed and his release broke free. Maddie felt the warmth of it inside her and instinctively clasped her thighs tighter around Nic's hips.

After a long moment Nic fell into an exhausted slump beside Maddie. He hugged her close, arms wrapped right around her. All he could think of before sleep and blackness claimed him was how intense it had felt to have no barrier to his release going deep into Maddie, and how tightly her legs had clasped him to her in that moment.

Maddie woke and looked at Nic. He was so much more relaxed in sleep. He was always so tightly controlled. Her heart lurched and she suddenly longed for a time when she would see him relax and smile…and laugh. Perhaps he would…with someone else. Not her. He'd been softer once—she'd seen it in his eyes, along with hope. But she was the reason that softness and hope had been replaced by cynicism. When she thought of how vulnerable he'd been when they'd met, underneath all his arrogance…her rejection must have cut too deep for him ever to forgive.

Maddie didn't want to wait for Nic to wake and react to her presence. She knew something had changed last night. They'd crossed a line. The past had been well and truly dealt with. This affair had always been about old scores, lingering desire… The contract had provided a kind of reprieve, but it would be signed soon and then Nic would be relegating Maddie back to the periphery of his life.

Maddie had to face up to her conscience, which was riven with guilt. She'd slept with Nic using the contract as an excuse because she'd believed that it was the only way she could sleep with him. He'd never have wanted her without the contract. He wouldn't have lowered himself to seduce her just for desire's sake.

She had to get out of there before she forgot that and started wishing and hoping that perhaps…in another world…if they hadn't shared such a tangled history… eveything might have been different.

The fact was that ultimately Nic had got his hands on the one thing he wanted most, and that was the Vasquez estate. In the end he'd prevailed, and got personal revenge into the bargain.

When Nic woke the sun was high outside and he felt completely disorientated. The bed was empty beside him and he closed his eyes. The bittersweet relief that went through him to find that he was alone was palpable.

The last thing he remembered was waking during the night and finding Maddie soft and sexily pliant in his arms.

He'd been hard and aching and she'd woken, pushing her buttocks against him, urging him to take her.

He'd slid into her from behind. It had been quiet and intense.

His head reeled anew when he thought of what Maddie had told him yesterday. He'd acted from some visceral place, bringing her back here to make love in a need to negate the awful words. When he recalled what it had been like to lock eyes with her as they'd made love he felt dizzy, even though he was lying down.

Maddie's revelations put a spin on the past that Nic wasn't sure he could really assimilate. Her reaction that day...he had no defence against it any more, nothing to hide behind. He knew he would have reacted exactly the same—might possibly have been even more brutal than she'd been to him. And the fact that she'd been burdened with the knowledge...it made Nic feel sick.

She'd wanted to see him again. If her mother hadn't told her what she had, the following day at the orchard would have been very different. A cold sweat broke out on Nic's brow as he lay there and contemplated how different things might have been...and could be now. And there his mind immediately shut down. His body was locked with tension.

He'd come full circle with Maddie. They'd reached a truce. He could forgive her now and move on. He'd invest in her estate, help her get back on her feet. And that had to be enough. He simply could not contemplate an alternative, because that meant challenging the walls of defence he'd needed to exist for so long. Since his mother had smothered him with anxiety and his father had brutalised him. And since he'd spent that week with Maddie and felt his heart beating for the first time...

The concept of love had been alien to him until he'd met

Maddie. And then it had become mangled, and had withered inside him after her cruel words and brutal rejection.
No matter what he knew about that day now, he couldn't
undo the damage. And Maddie was inextricably bound
up in all of that, so she could never be a part of his future.

Nic's bones ached when he thought of relegating Maddie
to his past. He jack-knifed off the bed and took a stinging
cold shower, assuring himself that finally he could move
on—but he could only do it by leaving Maddie behind.

Maddie walked out of the clinic feeling tired but happy.
Until she saw a familiar Jeep pull into the car park.
Unconsciously she started walking faster and put her head
down. She cursed when she heard, 'Maddie!'

Slowly she turned around. She didn't feel ready to face
Nic yet. It had been two days since she'd left his bed, and
she'd not seen him or heard from him. The message was
clear: it was time to move on.

She schooled her features into a bland, polite mask. But
still when she saw him she couldn't stop that impulse she
had to devour him with her eyes. Her heart spasmed, her
arms tight across her chest. 'Nic.'

'How is Maria?'

Maddie smiled tightly. 'She's going to be fine. The operation was a success. She'll need to recuperate here at the
clinic for a few days, but she's been very lucky. They're
very grateful to you.'

Nic waved a hand as if to brush aside the considerable
expenses he'd met for Maria's operation and care. 'It was
nothing,' he said gruffly.

Maddie's chest felt constricted. 'Was there something
else you wanted?'

He looked at her for a long moment, and she felt an icy
feeling of foreboding.

'The other night…we didn't use protection.'

Maddie went cold and then hot. She hadn't even thought about it afterwards. Mortified, she babbled, 'It's fine. I got my period today.'

Nic looked grim. 'That's good…'

Wanting to escape, Maddie said, 'Hernan is coming back to the estate tomorrow. He's going to check over the contract, so I should have it signed the day after, if he thinks it's okay.' Maddie felt like a fraud for delaying the inevitable: she'd looked over the contract and it was more than fair—and generous.

Nic nodded. 'I'll come and pick it up myself.'

'Goodbye, Nic.' Maddie turned quickly and headed straight to her Jeep, hating the stinging in her eyes. She knew it was silly, but somehow *now* felt like the moment when whatever link they'd shared for the past eight years was finally broken.

'Maddie—'

Maddie's steps faltered and her breath stopped. Blinking back the moisture in her eyes furiously, she turned around again. Nic hadn't moved. The planes of his face were stark, and he said, 'I'm sorry that—'

Maddie put up a hand, bile rising in her throat at the thought that he was going to give her some platitude. 'Don't, Nic. Just don't. You don't have to say anything. It's done.'

And she turned and half ran, half walked to her Jeep. She and Nic had been seeking some kind of closure and now they had it. Whatever she'd felt move between them the other night had been nothing more than an illusion, a reaction to heightened emotion.

So, she asked herself on the way home through a veil of tears, if this was closure why did it feel so *un*closed?

* * *

Maddie sat looking at the contract. It was early in the morning. She and Hernan had gone over it all last night and he'd concluded that she wouldn't have got a better deal from anyone else. With Nic's investment the entire estate and house would be completely renovated and updated—something her old-fashioned father had fought against all of his life. His resistance was one of the main reasons the estate had fallen apart.

Hernan and Maria would be well protected and looked after. Nic was going to bring in a project manager and a new head winemaker. He would also hire new cellar hands and seasonal grape-pickers, as well as the machinery needed to mass-pick grapes.

Maddie knew she had no choice but to accept this investment—not just for her sake but for the sake of the local economy. The Vasquez estate had long been an employer of locals and it could be again. Not to mention the huge debt she owed Hernan and Maria, who needed support now more than ever. She couldn't deny that she wanted the estate to flourish again. It was just a pity that she wouldn't be there to witness it.

With a heavy heart Maddie picked up a pen and signed on the dotted line. And in doing so she sealed her fate—because she couldn't remain here now. She couldn't renege on this deal, but she also couldn't go on living here, seeing Nic every day, living with his casual dismissal of their affair. She'd sold her soul and heart to him—and she'd used his investment in the estate as an excuse to hide behind.

What had happened between them amounted to nothing more than a ream of paper written in legalese.

Maddie tried to write a note to Nic, but no matter what she said it came out trite and ridiculous. In the end she gave up and simply wrote:

Nic, I am handing full control of the estate and all decisions to Hernan. He is the best person to oversee the work to be done.
Yours, Maddie.

Even that made her scowl. She folded it and put it in an envelope and left it on top of the contract, with her note to Hernan. And then she left her home.

Nic watched the dawn break, casting a pink light over the snow-capped Andes in the far distance. His jaw itched with stubble. His eyes stung. He hadn't slept all night. He hadn't slept since he'd woken in the empty bed the other morning.

The view he now looked upon, which encompassed the vastness of his estate, usually never failed to fill him with a sense of satisfaction, but for weeks now it had failed to move him. He'd become distracted and had lost interest in work—which had been his one *raison d'être* for ever.

Only yesterday Eduardo had had to repeat himself three times before Nic had registered what he was saying, and then Nic had snarled at him like a bear with a sore head. Nic had, of course, apologised profusely—he'd never lost his rag like that before—but the level of control he'd been wielding for years was deserting him spectacularly.

And Nic knew the moment it had started to desert him. When he'd seen Madalena Vasquez walk through the doorway in that hotel in Mendoza. He'd known *then*, even before he'd recognised her, that everything had changed irrevocably.

And just like that, as the pink light spread across the Andes, Nic knew what it meant—and what he had to do if he wanted to gain any sense of control or sanity back. All of this—his struggle with his parents, his health—meant absolutely nothing now. Because from the moment he'd seen Maddie Vasquez on her horse eight years ago and followed her to the orchard, she'd controlled his destiny.

She'd made him trust, and then she'd broken him apart and reformed him with her brutal rejection—which was now so understandable. But she was the only one who could heal him, make him take a chance on trusting again...

From the moment she'd come home he'd been slowly thawing, coming back to life inside and fighting it every step of the way. The pain of it was almost unbearable. But now that pain was as necessary to him as breathing.

Nic hadn't even realised he was moving until he was in his Jeep and driving out of his gate towards Maddie's estate. He barely noticed the one other vehicle on the road—a taxi. When he got to the house it felt silent, and Nic knew with a sick feeling why it felt like that.

He went into the study and saw the notes and the contract. He put the letter for Hernan aside and opened the one for him and read it. Slowly he put it down and picked up the contract. He looked at the last page. Maddie's name was scrawled on the bottom line.

With an inarticulate roar of rage Nic flung the contract against the book-lined wall and the pages went everywhere. He turned and stormed out, eyes wild.

Maddie shuffled forward in the queue at the ticket booth, counting her money. She had just enough. When she got to Buenos Aires she would try to persuade her aunt to let her stay for a couple of weeks while she tried to find a—

'Running away, Maddie?'

Maddie's brain froze mid-thought. She looked around to see Nic standing there, arms crossed across that broad chest. His calm and reasonable tone belied his wild look: his hair was messy, his eyes were bloodshot, and his jaw was stubbled with dark blond beard. And he was utterly, utterly gorgeous.

Maddie quickly turned back to face the queue again, and tried to will down the heat seeping into her cheeks. 'I don't know why you bothered to come here, Nic. And, no, I'm not running away.'

She went forward a few steps and Nic kept pace beside her.

'Could have fooled me. Did you realise you couldn't hack it? That you don't really care for your estate that much, after all?'

Maddie rounded on him, bristling. 'You *know* that's not true. I love that estate.'

'Then why are you leaving?'

Maddie flushed. She was becoming aware of people nudging each other, because inevitably they recognised one of Mendoza's foremost citizens. All they'd have to do was recognize *her* and then they'd have enough fodder to gossip about for months. *De Rojas has run Vasquez out of town!*

Reluctantly Maddie stepped out of the queue and moved away, so people couldn't hear them. She rounded on Nic. 'I don't need to be there for you to invest in the Vasquez estate.'

Nic was grim. 'It's part of the deal.'

Maddie felt like stamping her foot, and emotions weren't far from the surface. 'Nic, I'm leaving, and there's nothing you can do or say to stop me.'

Resolutely she turned to join the back of the queue and start again. Then she heard Nic say rawly from behind her, 'What if I said I don't want you to go, and it's got nothing to do with the investment?'

Maddie stopped, and her breath grew very shallow. She wasn't even aware of the interested eyes of onlookers flitting between her and Nic. She'd misheard him—or he didn't mean what she'd thought he meant.

She took an experimental step forward and heard, 'Maddie, *dammit.*'

And then Nic was in front of her, planting himself squarely in her way. She looked up. The muscle in his jaw was ticking.

'Nic...?'

'I don't want you to go because I've just realised how much I need you.'

Maddie's hands were gripping her bag. Something fluttered ominously in her chest but still she thought he had to be talking about the investment.

'But Hernan will be there. He can handle it...'

Nic nearly exploded. 'I'm not talking about the investment. I don't care about that. I only offered to invest because you seemed so determined to throw yourself in harm's way. And the contract—' Nic stopped abruptly and cursed out loud before admitting, 'The contract was a way for me to have you in my bed without admitting that I was terrified you'd reject me again.'

He reached out a hand and touched Maddie's cheek. She felt his hand trembling. *Déjà vu* washed over her.

'I messed up, Maddie, because I was too cowardly to admit how much it made me *feel* when you came back here.' He shook his head. 'Your rejection that day...it was like having my heart torn out of my chest and ground into the earth. Nothing mattered after that. I closed myself off. In the space of that week I fell for you so deeply...'

Maddie's vision was blurring. She brought her hand up over Nic's on her face and held it there, willing him to trust her. 'Oh, Nic...I'm so sorry that happened. That my mother poisoned my mind...that I couldn't tell you. I wanted you so badly. I fell for you too. And I know that's why you can't possibly forgive me.'

Resolutely Maddie took Nic's hand down and dropped it. She stood back. 'That's why I'm leaving. I'm not strong enough to live near you, loving you, knowing that you're getting on with your life…and you have to move on.'

Nic sounded slightly dazed. 'You love me? Even now?'

Maddie nodded and fresh tears blurred her vision. 'You were always in my heart and thoughts. I told myself when I came back that I hated you for being so autocratic, and for making me believe that what had happened between us eight years ago was pure lust on your part. But it was a lie. I agreed to that stupid contract because on some level I thought it was the only way you'd have me…'

Maddie looked down and wiped at her damp cheeks. She clutched her bag and took a step around Nic—only to feel him take her arm in a strong grip.

She couldn't even look at him. 'Please, Nic…let me go. You can't make me stay. Not now.'

He didn't listen. He turned her around and tipped her chin up. Maddie saw his face and her heart stopped. He looked young…and free of those awful shadows. A smile curled the corners of that beautiful mouth and her heart started again, making her feel light-headed.

Gently Nic asked, 'Have you listened to a word I've said?'

Maddie felt confused. What *had* he said?

Suddenly Nic took her bag out of her hand and dropped it to the ground. And then, before she could take in a breath, he was down on one knee in front of her, holding her hand in his.

Looking up at her with those intensely blue eyes, he said throatily, 'Maddie Vasquez, I love you. I was fascinated by you before I ever met you, and then when we did meet I fell deep into your heart. I've never stopped loving you, no matter how hurt I was, and I only realised that when you came back home. I told myself I hated you, that I wanted revenge...but I wanted *you*. And I wanted your heart. But I was too cowardly to admit it...'

Maddie was stunned into silence, sure that she had to be dreaming. The queue had long since broken up, and they were now surrounded by an avid crowd of spectators. Maddie heard someone close to her sigh theatrically.

'Maddie Vasquez...will you please marry me? I can't move on with my life unless I know you're going to be in it. I want us to have babies and grow old together, to be the ones to bury this ancient feud for ever. I love you.'

Maddie started crying in earnest, emotion rising up within her and making her shake. Nic stood up and pulled her into his arms, cradling her and soothing her. Eventually, when she could, she pulled back and looked up at him. He still looked wild, and trepidatious. She could see the old fear in his eyes—the fear that even now she'd walk away...

She reached up and put her arms around his neck.

She pressed a salty kiss to his mouth and said on an emotional sigh, 'Yes, I'll marry you, Nic de Rojas. How could I possibly do anything else when I love you so much?'

The cheers of the crowd made Maddie bury her head shyly in Nic's chest, and then she felt him lifting her into his arms and striding out into the glorious sunshine.

One year later

'No,' Nic said patiently. 'We *are* married, but my wife has an extensive estate in her own name so she decided to stay a Vasquez. She's a modern woman.'

Maddie's hand was tightly clasped in Nic's. She fought back giggles when he gripped it tighter and they watched the snooty older couple walk away, radiating disapproval at this unconventiality. The people of Mendoza were only slowly coming to terms with a de Rojas/Vasquez union, but the Vasquez estate was well on its way to flourishing again under its own label.

When the couple had gone Maddie laughed out loud, and buried her head in Nic's chest to hide it. His hand was tender on the back of her neck, fingers exerting a gentle pressure, and Maddie finally looked up when she'd collected herself, loving the feeling of languid heat which invaded her bones at his touch, which would turn to something much more urgent given half a chance—even more so now than it ever had.

'Well, Señor de Rojas.' She smiled up at her husband. 'Do you realise that this is our first anniversary?'

Nic frowned. 'But we only got married nine months ago...'

Maddie looked around the sumptuous ballroom of the hotel in Mendoza and squeezed his hand. 'Not that anniversary. I mean this time last year we met again for the first time...'

Nic looked down into his wife's clear and loving green gaze and felt his chest tighten almost unbearably. It happened a lot, this physical feeling of love. That night a year ago—he could remember seeing her shape in the doorway, could remember feeling right then that trouble was in store. And he wouldn't have changed one second of it.

He smiled and took her hand, lifting it to his mouth to kiss the inner palm. Her eyes darkened and immediately blood rushed to his groin. He almost groaned out loud. They were like two rampant teenagers.

His voice was low and husky. 'Happy anniversary, my love...'

Maddie turned her face into his palm and Nic glanced up and cursed softly, wishing that they were alone. He felt Maddie sigh against his hand and looked down, immediately concerned. He saw her wry look and felt her hand come between them, to rest on the very prominent swell of her belly. She was already two weeks overdue.

She grumbled good-naturedly, 'Do you think this baby will *ever* appear? If he takes much longer I'll need a crane to get around.'

Nic smiled wolfishly and wrapped both arms around Maddie, pulling her close. 'I can think of one way we can urge him along...'

Maddie's insides liquefied at the carnal look in Nic's eyes. This past year had been a dream. She loved this man more than she'd even allowed herself to believe possible when she'd first fallen for him.

Maddie asked, 'Can we just leave? Now?'

He pressed a kiss to her mouth and said, 'We can do whatever we want.'

'But your speech...'

Nic looked round and Maddie saw him share a look with Eduardo, his head winemaker. He looked back to Maddie. 'Eduardo will take over. This...' He put his hand possessively on her belly. 'You, *us*—there's nothing more important than that.'

The next day, at five p.m., Nic and Maddie welcomed their son, Alvaro, named after Maddie's brother, into the world.

Maddie, exhausted but happy, looked at Nic cradling his son—all ten pounds eleven ounces of him—and smiled wryly. 'If we could patent your particular method of helping labour along I think we could make a fortune.'

Nic's little finger was caught in a chubby hand, and he looked at his wife and said mock seriously, 'Next time I'll make sure to put much more effort in.'

Maddie groaned softly. 'The way I'm feeling right now, there won't *be* a next time.'

Nic chuckled, and Maddie was glad to see the colour restored to his face. He'd nearly fainted in the delivery room, his torture at being so helpless evident when Maddie was in such pain.

He came and handed Alvaro back to Maddie, who sat up and started to breastfeed. Nic leant close and whispered in her ear, 'Don't worry, Mrs Vasquez. I'll make it so pleasurable next time you won't even think about the pain.'

Maddie looked at Nic and saw how dark his eyes were at seeing her breast exposed like this, their baby suckling furiously. She felt a familiar tugging in her lower body that no pain could diminish—not even a fifteen-hour labour.

She groaned softly and said, 'What have I let myself in for?'

Nic pressed a kiss to her neck and then pulled back to look at her, one hand on his son's head. He just smiled.

* * * * *

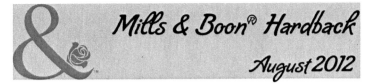

Mills & Boon® Hardback

August 2012

ROMANCE

MEDICAL

Mills & Boon® Large Print

August 2012

ROMANCE

A Deal at the Altar — Lynne Graham
Return of the Moralis Wife — Jacqueline Baird
Gianni's Pride — Kim Lawrence
Undone by His Touch — Annie West
The Cattle King's Bride — Margaret Way
New York's Finest Rebel — Trish Wylie
The Man Who Saw Her Beauty — Michelle Douglas
The Last Real Cowboy — Donna Alward
The Legend of de Marco — Abby Green
Stepping out of the Shadows — Robyn Donald
Deserving of His Diamonds? — Melanie Milburne

HISTORICAL

The Scandalous Lord Lanchester — Anne Herries
Highland Rogue, London Miss — Margaret Moore
His Compromised Countess — Deborah Hale
The Dragon and the Pearl — Jeannie Lin
Destitute On His Doorstep — Helen Dickson

MEDICAL

Sydney Harbour Hospital: Lily's Scandal — Marion Lennox
Sydney Harbour Hospital: Zoe's Baby — Alison Roberts
Gina's Little Secret — Jennifer Taylor
Taming the Lone Doc's Heart — Lucy Clark
The Runaway Nurse — Dianne Drake
The Baby Who Saved Dr Cynical — Connie Cox

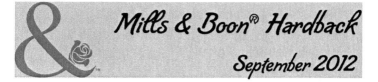

Mills & Boon® Hardback

September 2012

ROMANCE

Unlocking her Innocence	Lynne Graham
Santiago's Command	Kim Lawrence
His Reputation Precedes Him	Carole Mortimer
The Price of Retribution	Sara Craven
Just One Last Night	Helen Brooks
The Greek's Acquisition	Chantelle Shaw
The Husband She Never Knew	Kate Hewitt
When Only Diamonds Will Do	Lindsay Armstrong
The Couple Behind the Headlines	Lucy King
The Best Mistake of Her Life	Aimee Carson
The Valtieri Baby	Caroline Anderson
Slow Dance with the Sheriff	Nikki Logan
Bella's Impossible Boss	Michelle Douglas
The Tycoon's Secret Daughter	Susan Meier
She's So Over Him	Joss Wood
Return of the Last McKenna	Shirley Jump
Once a Playboy...	Kate Hardy
Challenging the Nurse's Rules	Janice Lynn

MEDICAL

Her Motherhood Wish	Anne Fraser
A Bond Between Strangers	Scarlet Wilson
The Sheikh and the Surrogate Mum	Meredith Webber
Tamed by her Brooding Boss	Joanna Neil

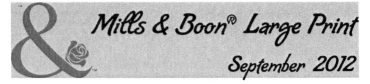

ROMANCE

A Vow of Obligation	Lynne Graham
Defying Drakon	Carole Mortimer
Playing the Greek's Game	Sharon Kendrick
One Night in Paradise	Maisey Yates
Valtieri's Bride	Caroline Anderson
The Nanny Who Kissed Her Boss	Barbara McMahon
Falling for Mr Mysterious	Barbara Hannay
The Last Woman He'd Ever Date	Liz Fielding
His Majesty's Mistake	Jane Porter
Duty and the Beast	Trish Morey
The Darkest of Secrets	Kate Hewitt

HISTORICAL

Lady Priscilla's Shameful Secret	Christine Merrill
Rake with a Frozen Heart	Marguerite Kaye
Miss Cameron's Fall from Grace	Helen Dickson
Society's Most Scandalous Rake	Isabelle Goddard
The Taming of the Rogue	Amanda McCabe

MEDICAL

Falling for the Sheikh She Shouldn't	Fiona McArthur
Dr Cinderella's Midnight Fling	Kate Hardy
Brought Together by Baby	Margaret McDonagh
One Month to Become a Mum	Louisa George
Sydney Harbour Hospital: Luca's Bad Girl	Amy Andrews
The Firebrand Who Unlocked His Heart	Anne Fraser

0812 GEN STD LP